3 Breaths

a novel by

LK COLLINS

Print Edition

Cover Design by Prezident Collins
Edited by Lisa Christman, Adept Edits
Formatting by Paul Salvette, BB eBooks
Photography by FXQuadro

"Take each breath as though
it could be your last."

– LK Collins

Dedication

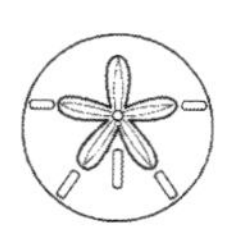

For my readers, this one is for you. Thank you for all of the years of support.

Prologue

"To Krane and Zoë," Logan says holding his beer high in the air. The room echoes in cheers and I raise my drink. He hops off the stage, letting the band get back to playing as Zoë breathes softly on my neck. The small gesture from her makes me horny as fuck. "I want you," she whispers, immediately filling my mind with images of fucking her.

Looking into her gorgeous eyes, I want her too. "I know," I respond, teasing her, and it makes her shake her head at me.

"You know, if you want to survive this engagement, you better start taking care of me."

She's joking, but the insinuation that I don't take care of her sets me off. She is my world and the only woman that I've ever loved. Swooping her tiny ass off of the ground, I toss her over my shoulder to "take care" of her, regardless if we're in a New York City bar or not. She screams, "Put me down, baby," and hits my back. No one seems to notice us, as the crowd is engrossed in the band that I'm sure Logan spent a ton of money on to play for us tonight – his parents are loaded and he definitely takes advantage.

"Oh, I'll put you down in just a minute." I slap her ass, kicking open the bathroom door. The single stall is open and there is just one guy in here. All I have to do is give him that look, that one that says *get the fuck out of here or I'll rip your head off* and he scatters.

I set Zoë down and she wobbles a little, running her fingers through her fucking hair, knowing what that does to me. "Don't do that."

"Why?" she asks, resting her hands back on one of the sinks.

"You know why."

She smiles and gestures me to her with one finger. We are both drunk – the connection we share is like nothing else, combine it with liquor and we are combustible. Looking into her eyes makes everything in my world complete. Knotting my fingers into the back of her hair, I press my lips to hers; she tastes like Patrón and Zoë, the perfect fucking combination.

She moans, wrapping her legs around me and runs her hands up my back, sending a shiver right to my cock. Dropping my hands, I grip her thighs and carry her to the door. Knowing that there's no lock on it, I'll have to fuck her right here to keep it shut. If it was anyone else but Zoë, I wouldn't give two shits if they saw us fuck.

Her tongue caresses mine, never letting up. My cock is so hard that it hurts. Pushing myself against her, I groan, needing to be inside her. "Let me down," she asks, needing it just as much as I do.

"Keep your back against the door," I tell her, pulling her tank top down and exposing her hard pink nipples. My mouth moves to them and I suck hard, flicking my tongue back and forth on one of my favorite parts of her body. She slides her jeans down her legs and then fumbles with mine. The tip of my dick is numb from straining against the rough fabric, throbbing for her.

Finally she sets my cock free and I let out a deep puff of air, looking down at her hand as she strokes my shaft. The sensation is one of the things I live for. Reaching down, I grab her wrist, along with her other one, pulling her arms above her head. She nudges her hips forward with her legs spread apart. I watch her begging me in her soft sexy voice, "Please fuck me." Still holding both of her hands with one of mine, I grip my cock with the other and nudge myself against her.

Fuck, she's wet.

Rubbing myself on her clit, she moans and rocks her hips even more. I love to play with her…to tease her. Especially when she's this turned on.

"Take back what you said."

"What do you mean?" she asks, breathless and confused.

"About me needing to *start* taking care of you."

"I take it back. You know I was joking, baby."

With a triumphant smirk on my face, I let go of her hands and lift her up again, knowing that I am too tall to fuck her while standing. She attaches to me and we both look down at my swollen dick as I gently nuzzle my way deep inside of her. Then locking eyes with her, everything in this moment freezes. She's panting as I begin to stroke myself inside of her and this makes me pick up my pace. The noise of her ass hitting the door echoes throughout the room.

Christ, her pussy is my heaven.

The door nudges a little and I press her into it, digging myself a little further into her cunt. “Occupied,” I growl.

“Sorry,” the person on the other side says. Zoë hangs on to my neck and I stroke myself inside of her, feeling her warmth and tightness. Loving what her body does to mine. Pressing my lips to her neck, I suck hard, feeling my cum brew.

“Fuck, baby,” she cries, and I pull away. Her skin is flushed and her eyes are closed. My balls tighten as she clamps her pussy down around me and I watch her fall from this world. Holding on to my orgasm for as long as possible, I watch her. Fuck, she is so gorgeous, the most beautiful thing that I have ever seen. She writhes and shakes against me as I shove myself into her as deep as I can.

Then…it hits me. I groan, pumping my cock ’til my cum shoots deep inside her. Gradually, I slow my movements and rest my forehead against hers.

“I love you, baby,” I tell her, easing my way

out of my favorite place.

"I love you," she responds and grabs a paper towel, cleaning herself off. I wrestle my dick back into my pants, holding the door closed. Watching her, I know that I could come a few more times, but that'll have to wait until we are home.

"Ready?" I ask, holding my hand out to her as she zips her pants.

"Yup," she says and grins at me walking out of the restroom. Intertwining my fingers with hers, I stop at the bar and get us two more beers. We both turn and look at the huge crowd of our closest friends.

"You know our engagement dinner with both sides of our family isn't gonna be this fun," she says.

"We'll make the best of it and have fun, like we always do, babe. Your mom will be drunk, so we'll be right there along with her."

Taking a swig of the beer the bartender hands me, I can't help but get lost in her beauty.

She takes a quick drink of her beer as I take her hand and lead her to the dance floor to dance with our friends and party the night away.

Ten beers, seven shots, and something else I can't remember later, it's time to leave. Everyone else is gone and Zoë is almost asleep in my arms.

"Let's go, you party animal."

She looks up at me with her hair in her face and all I can see are her teeth. I can't help but laugh – oh, she's going to be hurting tomorrow. Wrapping my arm around her, we stumble out into the cool spring night. The subway station is just a block away and after a fifteen-minute ride, we'll be home.

"You good?" I ask Zoë as we make the short walk.

"Uh huh," she responds, keeping up with me. The city is still buzzing; I swear New York never sleeps, and that's why I love it here. Entering the stairs for the subway, we begin to walk down and Zoë wobbles.

"Hold on to me, okay?" I prop her up as we make our way to the bottom.

"Mm hmm," she hums as her chin slumps toward her chest.

Waiting on the platform, there isn't anyone down here, except for a bum sleeping on a bench. The train pulls up and we enter the empty car.

Zoë flops down in a seat, her head still hanging low and I wonder if she's sleeping already.

Sitting next to her, I wrap an arm around her and she nuzzles to me.

"You okay?" I ask.

"Yeah. Baby?" she asks.

"Uh huh."

"Can we go to Long Beach tomorrow?"

"Sure," I respond, knowing she's not going to want to do anything but sleep all day, but being a smart man, I play along.

"I mean it."

"I know you do."

The subway zooms down the tracks rocking us back and forth a little, and I rest my head against hers. Zoning out on the orange and yellow seats across from us. Then, the alcohol sets in and my eyes close. My mind drifting back to fucking her in the bathroom.

Suddenly, my daydream is cut short. Zoë shakes violently in my hold.

"Baby," I yell holding on to her.

She doesn't respond, her eyes are rolled back in her head, and I know I have to do something. She has had seizures before, but not for a long time and never with me. I know I need to protect her until I can get help at the next stop.

Laying her on the floor of the subway, I cradle her head, her arms and legs flailing. My insides break, burning in pain watching her hurting like this. "Baby, please," I plead, crying, holding on to her, but she won't stop and I don't know what else to do. White foam pools out the sides of her mouth, followed by blood, and I fear she's bit her tongue.

"Zoë!" I scream, freaking out, watching her like this, so…helpless.

Finally her body starts to slow and my heart skips a beat. "Zoë, oh, baby," I weep, wiping my eyes so I can see her clearly and move around her. As I hover above her, she is still twitching a tiny bit and I wait for her to come to, cradling her head in my hands.

"Wake up," I whisper, resting my forehead against hers just wanting her body to calm. The announcement for the next stop goes off, so it's not long until I can get her off of here. My chest heaves watching her ragged breaths. She's struggling. "Baby, please hang in there," I whisper, looking at her as the train starts to slow.

Then her body settles and everything about her calms.

Thank God!

She's going to be okay! She has to be. I count

her breaths, waiting for her to come back to me. One…two…three…and then…nothing. I panic looking into her eyes – they are slightly open and glazed over. She is staring off, not looking at me. "No, Zoë!" I scream, shaking her by the shoulders. "You can't leave me!"

The train stops at the next station, and I scream for help when the doors open, even though I know it's too late. Looking down at her body, I knot my fingers into my hair, horrified. Her chest is still.

Tears cloud my vision as I lift her in my arms. Holding her lifeless body close to mine, I sit – crying – reeling in the agony of facing my greatest nightmare.

Everything around me spins.

Jesus, this cannot be real.

I sob into her neck, smelling her, my Zoë, my world, my everything…for one last time.

Chapter 1

Closing my eyes, I sit on the sand of Long Beach after another hellish run and breathe in the fresh sea air. My chest feels heavy, and I wish the pain from the run would erase my mind, but it doesn't.

I live in a constant hell.

The painstaking reality of my life is plagued with the images of Zoë dying in front of me. In my arms. I do my best to push those fucked up thoughts away and concentrate on what we had. That is if I can keep focused for long enough. Sometimes I can, and when that happens I can still smell her and picture her face – eyes – body – laugh, everything about her is at my fingertips, so close, but not close enough to reach. Even with the illusions that I hold on to, it's not enough. She's not here with me any longer.

I don't want to come to terms with the fact that I'll never see her again or touch her soft skin, but I have to, because she *is* truly gone. As fucked up as I am…I know what's real and what isn't. I will never feel her touch or her lips or look into her eyes. So for now, this is all that I have left, and it brings me as close to her as possible.

She might have unexpectedly left this world five months ago, but it still feels like yesterday in my head. The wound is fresh and burns me every minute of every day. The pain of losing her is like nothing that I've ever experienced. Every breath is brutal, my life really has zero purpose now, and it's hard to find a point to opening my eyes when I wake up each day. Everyone says with time things will get better, but I don't fucking buy that shit…it won't.

Listening to the sound of the waves as they crash against the shore, I wonder why God didn't take me, why her? There was no reason for it to be her time. The fucking doctors tell me that she died of SUDEP, Sudden Unexpected Death in Epilepsy, which in my mind is complete bullshit and confusing…maybe they think if they put a fucking acronym on it then it counts as an explanation. But it just means they don't know shit.

My phone rings and it pains me to open my eyes – I attribute that to exhaustion and the tequila that's still running through my veins from last night. Looking down at it through my dark shades, it's my mom, my overbearing and controlling mother. I know better than to blow her off; she'll just come find me if I do.

"Hey, Mom."

"How's the beach?" she asks, knowing that every morning I come here. I have since I lost Zoë, not able to bring myself to stop. I made her a promise before she died to bring her here and for that reason, this is where I feel the most connected to her.

"It's nice, Mom." There's an underlying aggravation to my tone. I really don't want to deal with her right now.

"Good, well, I just wanted to remind you of your sister's wedding and that you need to—"

"I know, Mom."

"Well, if you knew, you'd have gotten measured for your tux. Your dad's going now. If you wanna meet him, he can pay for it."

"Yeah, sure."

"I love you, Krane."

"You too." I hang up and lie back on the sand, closing my eyes.

Even though Zoë is gone, the connection that I feel to her here is so strong. I don't want to leave, I never do, but knowing my dad, he'll be pissed if I'm late. I get up and grab my towel, looking out at the vast horizon and the never-ending ocean.

Until tomorrow, beautiful.

Getting into my truck, I make the trip from Long Beach back to Oceanside, the town Zoë and I are from. I moved back here after I lost her. I couldn't bear to go back to our apartment in the city with all of her things in it…it was just too much. So I rented a small apartment and left everything as it was. Call me a coward, or whatever you want, but losing her has fucked me up in all sorts of ways.

Pulling onto the causeway to cross back over to the main land, a red sports car cuts me off. I slam on my horn and yell, "What the fuck, asshole?"

The short, bald driver throws a middle finger in the air and speeds off.

Fucking prick!

My blood boils; I want to follow him, to wring his fucking neck to take out some of the pent up aggression. I catch his dumb as fuck plate that reads FA5T. I put the pedal down as a text comes through my phone from Ivy, Zoë's sister. She's struggling just as badly as I am. Right away, I let up on the gas and read her words.

Do you have Zoë's iPod?

My world spins thinking of Zoë and her love for music. Glancing down at the old school, huge iPod that is plugged into my stereo, of course I have it.

Getting over the causeway, I come to a light and text her, ***Yeah, I do. Why?***

I continue on my way to meet my dad, waiting for Ivy, but she doesn't respond. Pulling up to the tailor's, I wish I had a bottle with me, so I could take a quick slam. I see my dad through the window dressed like he's already going to a fucking wedding. I spray myself with some Axe body spray and hope it masks the scent of last night's bender and my sweat from the beach.

Getting out, I run my hands over my hair in an attempt to tame it, but it's useless. My reflection in the glass door shows just how shitty I look. My clothes look like hell from picking them off of the floor after stumbling out of bed.

Proceeding inside, my dad turns to look at me, the disappointment is written all over his face. He and my mom don't understand why I am this way, but I really don't give a shit; they don't need to. They aren't me and don't have to live with the memories I do.

"Hey, Dad," I say, leaning in and hugging him.

"Son," he responds and pats my back. We pull away and I lift my sunglasses, the light from the inside of the store hurts my retinas, like a knife cutting through them. "Jesus Christ, Krane, you look horrible," he scolds me.

"Thanks, Dad." I know I look like crap, but it's like it'd kill the man to give me a fuckin' break every once in a while.

"What's going on with you?"

"Do you really have to ask?" I shake my head, feeling like I am about to lose control. "I'm fucking dying inside, Dad."

He walks outside and I put my sunglasses back on following him. He treats me like I'm a fucking kid when I'm almost thirty. I don't need to take shit like this from him. "Krane—"

I cut him off, "If you're gonna ream me,

fucking save it." I look off, waiting for his response.

"I'm concerned for you – you're my only son and you're not yourself right now. How long is this going to go on for? You're angry, you're drinking too much, and doing God only knows what else. What's it gonna take to snap you out of this?"

My mind recalibrates – he really has *no* idea the impact of what losing Zoë has done to me. "If you lost Mom, how would you be after a few months?"

"A few months, Krane, it's been almost six."

"I asked you a question," I bark back, since he's evading answering. He ponders my question, blinking a few times. I can see the look in his eye, and it's pissing me off. I need to leave before this escalates. I'm a loose fucking cannon, and if this goes further with him it won't help a thing.

"That's totally different."

"The fuck it is," I yell at him and walk off.

"Krane, wait!" he shouts, but I don't look back.

If he can't understand, then fuck him. I was with Zoë for years. She was my world, the only one who understood me. She stole my heart and tamed me when I was out of control. A lot like my mom did for my dad, so I thought he would understand, if anyone. But that's not the fucking case.

Chapter 2

"Can you be here in an hour?" Ling asks me.

I look around my empty apartment, like I have anything else to do. He knows I can be there whenever, so really the question is a moot point. Especially because fighting for him underground is my only source of income since I left the city and the life that Zoë and I had, where I was training every day with Logan. I used to have a plan to one day fight for a title, but that was before I lost it all.

"Yeah, the usual warehouse?"

"Yup."

"See you soon."

"Don't you wanna know who you're fighting?"

"Doesn't matter."

I hang up and look through my clothes for a pair of shorts. Everything is in a pile, the clean and dirty clothes have become mixed and I kind of have a recollection of doing some laundry last night, walking to the dryer, I'm stoked there's a clean load in it. Pulling out a pair of black ones, I toss them into my gym bag and then rummage through it to make sure I have everything else before I zip it up.

Opening the fridge, I grab a gallon of water from it and am thankful that I didn't drink too much today. Heading out, I load everything into my truck and make the trip into Jersey. Since it's illegal to fight in New York, I try to avoid it if I can. I don't care much if I am in jail or not, but if I land there, I can't drink, and that would probably force me to face a lot of demons that I'm just not ready to.

My phone rings and I answer it right as I begin to drive.

"Hello?" There is no response and I look at the screen. It's Ivy. "Just breathe, girl."

I hear her exhale and tell her, "Take your time; you know I'm not going anywhere." I watch the lights of the other cars pass me by, her quiet sobs faint on the other end of the line. Ivy is really the only person I've been able to relate to since losing Zoë. We've both been crushed by the loss.

"I..." she trails off and cries harder.

"Breathe, Ivy."

Deep sounds of air come through the phone and I know she's trying. To distract her from what has her so upset, I say, "Close your eyes, let's go somewhere together. What do you see?"

"Nothing."

"Come on, Ivy, you can do this, take us somewhere."

She's quiet and then finally whispers, "The jungle."

I chuckle at her, "Okay, the jungle, let me get there."

She laughs a little, I assume knowing my male brain was probably thinking something else. "What do you see?"

She sniffles a few times, thankfully calming down and I know my distraction tactic worked. "The sun is bright, everything is so green and beautiful."

"You always go to bright places," I tease her.

"It's better than some of the holes you've taken us to."

I recall a few of these similar conversations and it's true I have taken us down some dark roads. "So what's bothering you, girl?" I ask now that I have her attention diverted, keeping my eyes on the road.

"I found a card I got for Zoë. I got it for her when she got her last promotion at work, but I never sent it to her because I was too busy caring only about myself." She gets choked up. "God, Krane, I was such a terrible sister."

"Stop, you were not. Zoë loved you. Yeah, you guys had grown apart a little, but you were traveling so much with work and she was busy with the transition into the city. Sometimes life interferes, but that doesn't make you a terrible sister."

"Thanks for saying that, but I can't help but feel that way. It sucks that now I've figured out what's important…and she's gone."

Hearing her words, I wish I could figure things out myself. "What do you think Zoë would say?" I ask Ivy, hoping that she can shine some clarity on things for herself.

"She'd tell you to let her go, to move on with your life, and be happy."

"That wasn't what I was asking." She doesn't say anything else so I ask her, "I meant what would she tell you?"

"That she loves me, and always will…no matter what!"

"See, Ivy, those words you speak, you have to believe them too."

"I know…I just can't let go of the regret."

"You have to, for Zoë."

"I try, but—"

I cut her off. "Then you need to try harder."

"Okay," she whispers.

"Good! Listen, I hate to run, but I'm fighting tonight and just pulled up," I tell her.

"No worries, go. Thank you for calming me down. Stay safe."

We get off the phone and Ivy's words resound in my head, *Let her go, move on, and be happy.*

I don't believe that is what Zoë would say, but it doesn't matter what I think because she isn't here to tell me otherwise. Getting out of my car, I walk up to the back of the industrial warehouse where one of Ling's men watches the door. He nods his head at me and then opens it. I walk in, the sound of the crowd chanting and yelling echoes throughout the halls over another fight. Rounding the corner, I find my name on a paper taped to the door of the room that Ling usually has me change in.

He runs this place like a well-oiled machine. It's as close to legitimate as any underground fighting association can be. Except everyone here places bets on the fighters, so it gets rowdy and crazy at times. Going into fights now, I've got a different mentality than I did when Zoë was standing by my side. Fighting has become a means of survival. A way to release the blocked aggression and rage that lives inside of me.

I'm not fighting for a future or a career as I once dreamed of. I'm fighting to kill my opponent, to unleash upon him what the universe refuses to bear. Getting dressed, I sit on the bench and begin to wrap my knuckles. As I look down at my hands, I stretch the white tape, and there's a knock on the door.

"Come in," I call out and Ling pops his head in.

"What's up, man?" he asks.

"Not much, just wrapping up," I respond, raising my fist to him.

"Do you need anything?" he asks. I shake my head.

"Do you have someone to be in your corner?"

"Nah, but I'm good, it won't go past the first

round."

He laughs out loud. "You don't even know who you're fighting."

"Told you, doesn't matter."

He nods his head. "Okay, I'll have Bo stand by, in case it does go into the second round."

I raise my chin in agreement as he leaves and finish up wrapping my hands. Looking down at them, they look pretty shitty. But this isn't my forte; Logan always used to do it for me. But that's all in the past; I turned my back on him and everyone else that helped me out to try and achieve my dream, the night I lost Zoë. Which is really for the best. They don't need me bringing them down. Especially Logan – he's got a bright future ahead of him and doesn't need to waste it trying to help me. No one can help anymore.

Standing up, I stretch to get my body ready, then air box to get my heart racing. Two quick raps sound on the door and Bo pops his head in. "Ready, man?"

"Yeah." I grab my jug of water from the floor and he takes it from me. Fucking Ling probably told him to stay in my corner the entire night. Regardless, the moment that bell dings, all I see is red.

Walking out, I keep my eyes on the cage and look for my opponent. Fighting is just as much mental as anything else. Once I see him, everything changes. I want nothing more than to rip his head off, demolish him in the ring, and make him feel some of the pain that I do.

The crowd cheers upon my entrance. I've fought for Ling a dozen times and he says that I bring in the most revenue. Doesn't make much of a difference to me. The ref stops me before I enter the cage, checking my hands, to make sure they are wrapped properly. Then I show him my teeth to prove that I have a mouthpiece in, jogging in place, antsy, angry, needing to fight.

Once he gives me the go ahead, I run into the ring and right up to my opponent, catching him off guard as I tower over him and press my forehead against his, looking into his beady little eyes.

The ref pulls me away and the crowd cheers as I lunge back at him. But I'm stopped by a hand in the middle of my chest. I stand there waiting as we are both introduced and the rules are called. I feel like I am growling, waiting, like a beast is about to break out of me.

Then the bell sounds and I lunge at him

again, swinging viciously. He ducks and bobs my hits; little fucker is quick. Backing away, I need to play this smart and keep myself in control. Using my footwork, I can hear Logan's words as he used to yell at me when we would train together. *Let up a little, make this guy feel safer.* He weaves back and forth like a fucking boxer and I wait for him to attack. The crowd is screaming, and I notice he isn't really picking up his feet. Kicking as hard as I can, I connect with both of his legs and bring him down.

The room echoes and I scamper on top of him, laying hit after hit. The sensation each impact sends through my system is fucking amazing. So exhilarating. But it's fleeting relief from the pain and agony that is my life, because I know its release will end the second the fight does. His eye busts open, and blood pours from it. However, I don't let up knowing the ref will call it soon and I only want to enjoy this moment.

So I stand, like I'm giving him the chance to get up…he blinks a few times clearing his vision as I take my elbow, throwing it down hard on his nose. Blood spews from it and the ref gets between us. I look back at him waving his arms as he calls the fight and then I walk off.

The crowd screams for me, but the satisfaction of the win is nothing. As I scan the crowd, I'm reminded that Zoë is not here and quickly my reality sinks in. The three minutes of fighting made me forget things briefly, but it's just a band-aid like everything else in my life right now. It's a temporary fix, but…all I have.

Chapter 3

Sitting back on my couch, I look down at the half consumed bottle of tequila and Zoë's engagement ring on the table in front of me. I run my hands over my face as I get up and head into the bathroom. Christ, I look like shit. Staring at my drunken reflection in the mirror, I turn on the water and splash some on my face before running it through my hair. I haven't been sleeping for shit; the pain seems to never stop.

Heading back to the living room, I stare at Zoë's ring and know I need to get out of here. If I sit here and stare at it any more, I'll go fuckin' crazy. It's late enough, so Ling won't be calling me to fight tonight. Grabbing my phone and wallet, I contemplate where to go. As I walk down the stairs and out of my building, I decide on the bar just down the street from here. With my hands in my pockets, I walk letting the cool air run through me.

Zoë and I used to go here before we moved to the city. I can remember walking this same route with her. Approaching the bar, it's not that busy and then I notice the same red sports car with the dumbass FA5T license plate that cut me off the other day.

The wheels inside of my head start to spin – anything to take my mind off of Zoë I'm all about. Walking into the dimly lit establishment, Hazel, the usual bartender, notices me and smiles. I give her a wave and take a seat on one of the open bar stools. "What's up?" she asks, passing me a Budweiser and then pouring me a shot of tequila.

"Not much, you?"

She spans her hand outwards towards the patrons scattered through the bar. "Just this," she says. I drink to her comment, tipping my beer back at her as I set it down. "You doing okay?" she asks.

I shrug my shoulders, not wanting to talk about things, and raise the shot before knocking it back. She glares at me, and knowing Hazel isn't one to drop things, I nod my head. "I'm doing okay." She smiles at me. "Hey, do you know whose red flashy douchemobile is out front?"

She points to a group of guys playing pool in the corner. "I think it's the one with the shaved head. I saw him pull up when I was coming in tonight."

"Fucking prick cut me off the other day."

"Sounds like him; he seems to be an asshole, making his girlfriend get his drinks all night." I notice a girl sitting behind him texting on her phone.

"Is that her?" I ask, pointing.

"Yup."

She has short black hair and looks miserable, poor girl. She takes a drink of a Bud Light and I turn back to Hazel. "Will you give me a Bud Light, please?"

"Fuck no," she hollers, knowing what I'm up to. "I already covered for you last week."

"I'll take this one outside, I promise." Hazel knew Zoë – we all went to school together – so on some level she can relate to what I'm going through as she lost her too. That's why she accepts this fucked up drunken rut I'm in. She shakes her head not agreeing with me, but still hands me a Bud Light; I knew she couldn't say no.

Getting up, I take my beer and the girl's with me and walk right towards the douchebag's miserable girlfriend. Plastering the best smirk on my face, I tip the beer towards her and she looks up at me caught off guard. "A real man would never make you get your own drink, sweetheart."

She smiles at me and reaches for the beer. I give it to her and can sense eyes on the back of me. Holding true to my promise, I walk out the front door and head towards the dumbass' red car.

"Where the fuck are you going?" a whiny male voice says from behind. I take a swig from my beer as I make the last few steps and turn around, hopping up onto the trunk of his stupid car. Watching him and his two friends look at me stunned.

"Get off my car, asshole."

"Or what?" I challenge.

"Or I'll make you." He and his friends don't look like they can do shit. I'd love to fight all three of them. I'd put a good ass beating on all of them at once.

Taking the last chug of my beer, I lean forward and rest my elbows on my knees, tapping the bottle on his car. "I'm waiting, motherfuckers." I raise my eyebrows and can see that he's about to snap.

He lunges towards me, and with the bottle gripped by the neck, I strike it over his head. The glass shatters with a loud, satisfying pop, and he falls to the ground, his two friends standing there frozen, looking at me. "Come on, bring it, you pussies!" I yell with adrenaline pumping, but they back away and then his girlfriend comes running out panicked when she sees him on the ground. If he wasn't knocked out cold, I'd lay into him, but looking at his face…he's taking a nap, poor guy must have been tired.

I walk away and give Hazel a wave on the way back to my apartment as she stands at the entrance to the bar. She looks at me dumbfounded and just shakes her head. It's time for me to get home. I don't feel like dealing with the cops over this shit.

Chapter 4

"Krane, you really need to be eating more," my mom says as she fills my plate with a bountiful helping of eggs.

I look down at the yellow slimy mess and know she's right. But I lose my appetite when the reason why I haven't been eating much hits me.

"I've been eating, Mom, I promise."

She puts the pan in the sink and looks at me, leaning over the breakfast bar. "Your dad told me you guys got into it. We're both worried about you, baby." I set my fork on the ceramic plate and look her in the eye. "You need to talk about what happened," she pleads.

"What do you want me to say, Mom?" I ask her completely frustrated. "Zoë died in my arms and I couldn't do a damn thing to save her. Without her, I don't care about my life, bottom-fucking-line. I can't just get over that like everyone else wants me to. Every time I close my eyes, I'm haunted by those visions."

Tears gloss over my mom's eyes. I haven't spoken about what happened to Zoë except to the cops on the night that she passed. Revisiting the events breaks me and I'm about to lose control. Leaning into my mom, I kiss her forehead holding on to the back of her head and then flee her house.

I can't do this.

She sobs as I leave her and I feel terrible, but there's nothing more that can be said. I'm tired of other people telling me how to be, how to move on. This is my life and I'll fuckin' handle it the way that I need to. Driving home, I'm agitated, lost. My mind is haunted with horrific images of the worst day of my life, and somehow I end up at Ivy's work.

Staring out the window, I'm not sure why I am here, or how she can help. But I know she won't judge me. The feelings inside of me right now are fucked up and she's the only one that gets my pain. Sending her a text I ask, ***Can you take a quick break and come outside?***

She doesn't respond and I feel like it's wrong of me to burden her with my problems when she's working. This has all been so hard on her as well. It's been tough for her to even come back to work. Putting my truck in reverse, I look around me before backing out and she is walking out of the building. I stop right away, putting the vehicle in park and unlock the doors.

She hops in and looks exhausted. "You okay?" she asks, worrying about me immediately.

I run my hands over my face and let out a deep, frustrated sigh. "Just breathe," she says using my own words.

I stop what I'm doing and look at her out of the corner of my eye. I give her a small smile and say, "I don't know what to do anymore, Ivy. I get up every day and try to find a purpose for why I am here, but…" I trail off, anguished with the current mental state that I am in.

"Krane, it's not your job to figure out why you're here and Zoë isn't. You have to believe that it was her time." She rests her head back, her soft hair blowing from the air conditioner.

God, she is so strong. "How do you keep going on like you do?"

"I don't have much of a choice. I stayed in bed for over a month and was about to lose my job. Work keeps me busy, a good distraction, I guess. Have you thought about going back to the city and training with Logan?" she asks me.

I shake my head. "Without Zoë, I don't think that I can go back to my old life."

She reaches for my hand and grabs it, resting both of our hands on my thigh. "You need to start healing, for Zoë. She wouldn't want you to be like this."

I nod, acknowledging her words, but not having a clue how to do that. "Let's work out tonight. We can go to the gym at my apartment and just do a light workout. Maybe it'll help clear your mind."

I agree, for some God unknown reason. A social workout is the last thing I want. Oblivion is the only thing calling my name. But maybe being around Ivy reminds me of Zoë in a good way. Or maybe I'm just too fucked up to make a decision on my own right now.

"Good, I'm off at seven. Now, go home and nap; you look exhausted," she says.

I nod my head and hug her as she leans over, the warmth of her body so soothing. "I'll text you," she says and I watch her get out of my car. She's wearing tight pants and my eyes follow her ass as she's walking away.

Heading home, I'm shredded by guilt from staring at Ivy's ass, defiling her memory for noticing any ass not Zoë's, knowing she'd have my head on a fucking platter for checking out another chick, and probably take my head off that platter and run it through a meat grinder for it being her sister's. And then a bolt of agony shoots through me…all I want is Zoë. So much. So I stop to pick up a bottle of tequila to numb the pain and the shame. It's not the right thing to do…but right now, nothing that I'm doing is right.

Getting back to my car, I hear my name being called from behind me. "Krane, wait up, man."

I turn to see Rod, an old friend of mine that I partied with a ton before things with Zoë got serious and haven't really seen much since, but he knows all of what went down. "How the fuck are you?" he asks. "You holding up okay?" There is a genuine smile on his face, which is unlike Rod's egotistical self.

Looking down at the pavement, I kick the gravel frustrated, knowing it's better to just lie to him and tell him that I'm fine than to tell him how I really am. "You good, bro?"

"Yeah," I feign, not able to bring myself to look at him.

"Good! I'm glad I ran into you. I know you're going through a lot, but I wanted to invite you to a little get together at my place tonight. I'd love to hang out again and catch up. Like the old days."

I nod my head, picturing the nights that ended in blackout and nothingness we used to have together. "Yeah, man, for sure."

"Great, six o'clock?"

I agree and watch him jog back to his Mercedes. It's been years since we've hung out. Zoë hated Rod. He was a bad influence on me for sure. He always had sick ass parties and there was sure to be more than just booze there. Looking down at the handle of tequila I'm holding, something more might be just what I need right now.

Chapter 5

Do you want to grab a quick bite to eat before we work out? Ivy texts me.

Fuck! I completely forgot that I'd made plans with her tonight. Running my fingers through my hair, I think about how to handle things. Checking the clock, I figure the best thing to do is just ignore her, especially with the thoughts that I had earlier. She's Zoë's sister – her ass needs to be fucking nonexistent to me. But she is the only one who understands me, so I'll handle dealing with the repercussions tomorrow.

Sitting out front of Rod's familiar oceanfront house, my mind is flooded with so many memories of past times being here and none of them were with Zoë. That's strange to me, but also kind of a relief, because all of my memories lately have been consumed by the times we shared. Looking at my empty passenger seat, it hurts to not have her with me, though she sure as fuck wouldn't want to be here. Taking another swig of liquid brain eraser, I make myself one promise – tonight I will not think of Zoë and everything I lost…only the future, as dismal as it may seem currently.

Getting out of my car, I cross the barren street, music from his house pumping through the air. Walking up the front walk, the door is open and there are a ton of people scattered across the front. I head in and look for Rod, but instead spot a keg in the corner of the room. I fill myself a cup and plan to spend a lot of my night right here.

"What's up, man?" Rod says, coming in from outside.

I smile and raise my cup to him. "Not much, just got here."

"Don't drink that shit, let me get something for you," he says.

I finish the beer because for me any booze is good. Rod opens the freezer and pulls out a bottle of Patrón. It's not only my favorite, but his too. Pouring us each a glass of the chilled liquid he says, "I'm glad you made it tonight."

We head to the outdoor fire pit that is surrounded by a group of people, fortunately all strangers to me. As we each take a chair, I make an effort at small talk, when all I want to do is down my entire glass and let the booze take over. "What's the celebration for?" I ask.

"Nothing really, you know me, I just wanted to get some friends together and party."

Yup, that sounds just like Rod, always partying for no good reason. "You still fighting?"

"A little…" But I lose track of my words as my thoughts are interrupted. My eyes are glued to the door where an ex-girlfriend and her punk ass boyfriend she cheated on me with walk through.

Rod looks at me, catching sight of why I stopped talking and says, "Ahhh, fuck, man. I had no idea they were gonna be here."

"It's cool," I tell him, not giving a shit really. What she and I went through was so many years ago I couldn't care less. But for some reason, I can't take my eyes off of them. She doesn't look happy like I remember her, and he's not even acknowledging her, busy on his phone, completely oblivious to the world.

"Is it cool?" Rod asks me.

"For sure, brother. I wouldn't cause problems at your house. Plus, that's old news."

"Good. So when's your next fight?" he asks me, trying to pull me away from my death stare.

"Fuck, I don't know, it could be tonight. I'm doing more of the underground stuff right now." Taking a drink I sit back and look him in the eye. "I haven't really got back into taking it very serious since I lost Zoë. Nothing seems to motivate me anymore."

"I'm sorry, bro, I really am. But getting signed and fighting for a title was always what you were after. I'm surprised you aren't leaning on that now, going all out."

I shake my head, "I'm not doing much anymore but making it through each day."

He raises his drink to me. "I hear ya, but I can see it in you, man; you need to get back in it."

"Nah, if I don't have her to enjoy it with, it doesn't seem worth it."

"Well, some pussy then, something's gotta give to get you out of this fucked up rut."

I laugh and blow Rod off, like I have so many times through the years. He always thinks he knows what's best for other people.

He heads inside and I can't help my eyes as

they wander back to Jenn. She's looking at me, and her asshat of a boyfriend still has his nose in his phone.

Is that what she really wanted?

She smiles, but I can't do the same. Jenn really fucked me up and put me through a world of hurt. Now she has the audacity to smile sitting there with the asshole that she played me with, while I did nothing but love her. Looking at the two of them, I guess she got what she deserved.

What she did jacked with me, and Zoë was the only girl that could pull me out of the craziness that I was living in afterwards. Taking the last chug of my tequila, I head inside. The party is rowdy. Music fills the air and there are cheers around the keg. A girl is high in the air and everyone is chanting, "Drink, drink, drink, drink."

Filling up my glass with more Patrón, I lean back and watch these stupid people, knowing these guys are getting these girls drunk so they can get some pussy at the end of the night. My mind drifts to Jenn and I look outside to see her boyfriend finally paying her some attention. I can remember the night that I caught those two together, I wanted to beat the shit out of him, but she wouldn't let me. Looking at her now, I can't forget what she did to me. As I take a mouthful of alcohol, I catch sight of a familiar blonde. Zoning in on who it is, I'm shocked to see Jenn's little sister, Casey, and she's definitely not little anymore.

Damn, she's fucking hot.

Long blonde hair, tight ass, short belly shirt and then the group of people around the keg raise her high into the air and the chant begins again. Slamming my drink, I walk over to her and give the douchebag holding her legs a glare. He passes her legs to me and I watch her plump pink lips as they are sucked around the end of the tap.

The room spins a little and my cock twitches for the first time in a while.

Yup, I'm fucked up!

After she consumes what seems like a pitcher of beer, I set her down and pull her to me. Casey always had a thing for me and her reaction tells me that after all of these years that hasn't changed.

"Holy fuck, Krane!" she yells, throwing her arms around my neck. I hold her back keeping my hands low and whisper into her ear, "Fuck, you've grown up."

She pulls back with a grin ear to ear. "I'm twenty-three, what'd you expect?"

Running my fingers through my hair, I shake my head admiring her. She bites her bottom lip and I smirk at her. "Wanna have a drink with me, since you're legal and all now?"

She nods her head and I grab her hand, leading her to the bar where I grab the bottle of Patrón and pour us each a glass. "How have you been?" she asks.

I shrug my shoulders ignoring her question. "How 'bout you? What have you been up to?"

"Working. I got a job with a record label in the city and I love it." She takes a drink and looks outside. Then suddenly she grabs my hand and the Patrón pulling me away from the bar. She opens the door to Rod's spare bedroom and shuts it quickly.

"What the fuck, Casey! What's the matter?" I ask.

"Jenn was coming inside. Her reaction would be nuclear if she saw us together." Pushing the lock on the door to keep us safe, she takes a swig from the bottle and then passes it to me.

She wobbles a little and I hold her up. "You okay?"

"Yeah," she responds and catches me off guard cupping my dick through my pants. My eyes get wide and I set the Patrón on the dresser next to me. Looking at her as I rest one hand on the small of her back and the other I place behind her head, I let her keep touching me and find I like the feeling.

As she rubs my cock, I can't help but push myself into her, meeting her movements. She looks up at me with those innocent eyes and I bring our lips together. As our mouths connect, everything else in my mind slips away and my cocks throbs, leading me through this.

Kissing her, she moans as our tongues work together. I reach down with one hand, unbuttoning my pants, needing more. Slowly, she slides the zipper down and works her small hand around my needy shaft.

Pulling away from her kisses, I look to see her hold me so tightly and then she's on her knees. Brushing the hair out of her face, I let her take the lead, stretching those plump pink lips around me. Her warmth shakes my body, my balls tighten, and I work my hips matching her strokes. She swirls her tongue and my cock gets rock hard, sucking me off like I'm a fucking lollipop.

But before I blow my load, I pull away and bring her to her feet. She looks a little confused and asks, "Why did you stop me?"

"Because I want to please you too." Grabbing the hem of her shirt, I lift it above her head. Her tits spring free, pink nipples just like her lips, and I reach for her pants, unbuttoning them one button at a time. She stops me, grabbing my forearms and asks, "Do you have protection?"

It's not exactly where I imagined things going, but envisioning my cock inside of her, I know I need it. I nod my head and guide her onto the bed, drenching her entire body with kisses. "Does that mean you want my cock inside of you?" I ask her.

"Yes," she answers breathlessly.

Kissing and sucking on every part of her body, I am surprised with how clear my mind is and that nothing else matters right now. All I want to do is this, kiss her, lick her, suck on her, and then work her pussy. Teasing her nipples, she arches her body back, and I reach into the nightstand pulling out a condom, knowing Rod always has a stash in here.

Some things never change.

Tearing open the package, I kneel up and roll it down my length. She watches me with her legs spread wide waiting for me. Holding her legs apart, I hover over her, teasing her clit with the head of my shaft. Then slowly, I ease my way into her tight cunt. I've always been a sucker for a tight pussy.

Finding her mouth with mine, I kiss her slowly, synching my tongue to my thrusts. Casey moans, making me drill her that much more. Clearly, she must like it rough, because the deeper I get, the louder her noises are. Her legs are now wound around me and I find my hands in her hair.

My body trembles on top of her, enjoying this, a desire that I have missed. I support myself above her, working my thick shaft in and out of her. She arches back and I watch her, taking in her enjoyment of me. Then out of nowhere she screams my name and my balls erupt, shooting cum from the tip of my dick. I ride her hard. Loving how she quivers underneath me as we come together.

Casey is panting and we are both sweaty. I smirk, kissing her one more time before I pull my cock from her. "Fuck, you have a tight pussy."

She laughs lying on the bed naked. "And you have a great dick."

She stands briefly, grabbing the bottle of Patrón and takes a swig. I flush the condom and then come out of the bathroom to get dressed.

"Thank you," I tell her as she hands me the bottle.

I take a swig and she asks, "For what? The sex or tequila?"

"Both," I tell her and lean down giving her another kiss and pass the bottle back to her. She takes it from me and as I leave the room, she says, "You know, he's nothing like you were to Jenn. He's been an asshole to her for years."

I look back at her before I close the door and say, "I guess she got what she paid for."

I leave the room with the vision of her sitting naked on the bed etched into my brain. As I turn to head down the hallway, I run right into Jenn who looks concerned and asks me, "Have you seen my sister?"

I can't help but smirk at her.

Oh the timing.

I open the door and Casey is pulling up her jeans, her tits are still free and she stands in the room half naked and a little wobbly. Jenn looks at me and I wink at her before walking off. There are so many things that I could say to her right now, but it's pointless. Jenn always questioned things with Casey and I when we were together, so this will just rub salt into the old wound and hurt her. God, the look on her face was satisfying and fucking Casey took my mind off of the pain, just like fighting does.

Chapter 6

Fuck, I wish the banging in my head would stop. But it won't. Every time that I think it will, it keeps pounding again and again. "Krane," I hear my name and open my eyes, the light of day blinding me. "Krane, open up!"

I stumble from the couch, still drunk, and open the door. Standing so beautifully with two coffees and a brown bag in hand is Ivy. She turns her head from me and says, "Fuck, at least put some pants on."

I look down at my half hard cock and cover it with one hand. "Sorry," I say and turn searching for my jeans which are nowhere in sight. Walking towards the bedroom, I spot them on the floor and look back to see Ivy staring at my ass. "You can come in, Ivy."

She shakes her head as if to clear some bad thoughts from it and I laugh to myself, putting my jeans on. I look for my shirt and remember that I jerked off in it when I got home; thinking of fucking Casey got me going.

Picking another shirt out of my closet, I walk back out into the living room where Ivy is sitting on the couch, taking the food from the bag. "What happened last night?" she asks.

And I'm reminded that I completely blew her off. I trust that she really doesn't want to know what happened, so I lie. "Uhh, I got called to fight in the city and my fucking cell phone died. See?" I show her the black screen, knowing that I am horrible with charging the piece of shit, 'cause Zoë always did that for me.

"Did you win?" she asks.

"Yup, took him to the ground and snapped his arm in an arm-bar before the ref could call it."

"God, that's crazy. No wonder your face looks so good."

"You like my face, do you?" I tease her.

She slaps my arm and I raise my hands signaling a truce, and say, "I was only joking."

She nods and passes me a breakfast sandwich. "Thank you," I say.

"Of course." She looks away from me and I

worry that something is bothering her.

"What's the matter?"

"Nothing, I just…I had a rough night last night, again."

"Ivy, you gotta let it go. Each day, you have to focus on you. We can't keep telling the other to do one thing and not do it ourselves."

She nods a few times, listening to me, and takes a sip of her coffee. "I'm trying, but I had a horrible dream last night about her dying and now I just keep envisioning her that way. It's like that's the only way I remember her now."

"No, Ivy. You can't do that. She deserves more from you. It was a dream. Push it away. It's not real."

"I know, but it's like it's burned into my mind," she responds with tears in her eyes staring at the carpet.

Taking her coffee, I set it down and grab both of her hands. "Look at me."

Her pain-filled eyes are red and glassy and I just want to take her pain away. Then I get an idea, something that might help. "Come with me and let me show you something?" She looks confused, but nods her head, and I place our food back in the bag and the coffees in the tray.

Grabbing her hand, I lead her outside and down to my truck. "Where are we going?" she asks me as I help her up.

"It's better if I show you."

She buckles her seatbelt and I hand her the tray. She sets it on her lap and I jog around the vehicle. Getting in, my head is still pounding, but I know the fresh air and sound of the waves will help me, like it does every day.

We make the trek to Long Beach, Zoë's favorite place in the entire world, and I park in my usual spot. Ivy looks out the window and says, "I'm not really dressed for the beach."

"Me neither, just come with me." I grab a towel from my back seat and tuck it under my arm. Taking the food from her, we step onto the soft white sand. I never told Ivy or anyone that Zoë asked me to bring her here before she died. My mom knows I go to Long Beach every day, but she thinks it's just to clear my mind.

Seagulls swirl in the air and a few families are scattered around enjoying a day in this amazing place. "This was Zoë's favorite beach," I tell Ivy and hand her a sandwich, laying the towel down. We each remove our flip-flops and sit side by side, facing the water.

Ivy looks out at the expansive sea, letting out a deep breath of air that she has been holding. "We used to come here as kids for family vacations," she says.

"I know," I respond, "She told me…every summer."

"Yup. Do you come here often?" she asks me.

"Every day."

She looks at me a bit perplexed and asks, "Why?"

I stretch my legs out and lean back on my arms in preparation to go back to that place, the one place I hate to revisit. "The night Zoë…passed…" Tears fill my eyes, imagining her so helpless as she fought for her life. "She…she had asked me to bring her here the next day. I promised I would and even being in so much pain after losing her, I came. And have every day since. It's the place that I feel closest to her." Pain reels through me, reliving the events, and I finally pull my eyes away from the water, glancing at Ivy who is quiet. She is crying herself watching the waves.

I hoped bringing her here would help, but it seems to have only hurt her more. Taking my arm, I sling it over her shoulder and hug her tight against my body. She clings to me crying and I hold her close to me, where both of us can just…be.

Chapter 7

"Thank you for today," Ivy says, as she gets into her car.

"Of course, I hope it helped."

"It did. You always do, Krane." She looks at me with those eyes and I smile. Heading back into my apartment, I plug my phone in to charge it and turn the shower on. Looking around at the filth I call home, I collect the clothes that are littered around my house and toss them into the wash. The wedding is soon and I don't want to catch flak from my sister or family, which I know will happen if I pack a bunch of dirty crap.

Hopping in the shower, I let the hot water burn my skin and know that if I continue my endurance training like I have, I can keep doing underground fighting. That's really the only thing I know to do to get enough money to survive. And that's all I do anymore – survive.

As the water rolls down my body and washes away the pussy and booze of last night, I find myself thinking of standing at my front door naked with Ivy staring at me. I chuckle rinsing off. She always brings a smile to me. After getting out, I look in my closet for anything to wear and find a pair of shorts. In the distance, I hear my phone ringing. I walk out to it and pick it up, shocked by the name on the screen – Logan. I thought he'd have given up on me by now. I'm not sure what to say to him, so I'm glad it goes to voicemail.

Just as I walk away, a message chimes, and as much as I want to ignore it, I have to listen to it. "What up, Krane, it's Logan. I hope you're good, man." He pauses and clears his throat. "Listen, I wanted to let you know I'm having a barbecue on the beach tonight for my birthday. It would be cool if you could swing by. No questions from anyone or anything like that, I just miss you, buddy. It starts at six at Atlantic Beach."

The message comes to an end and the desperation in Logan's voice hits me hard. I haven't talked to him since the funeral. He was my best friend and I shut him out, just like I have everyone else that was in my life when Zoë died.

When I left the city, I left my old life and everything that was a part of it behind. I moved away from them and convinced myself that they were better off without me around, when really I couldn't bear the weight of their grief and the constant reminders of Zoë. It was a selfish thing to do and I knew that, but being alone and drunk was so much easier to make it through the days, rather than being fake and facing the demons that I'm still scared of. Taking a seat on my couch, I stare at the remnants of my life. Alcohol-filled nights to wash away the pain and a random fight here and there are all that I have to look forward to.

Heading out on the balcony, I decide to call Ivy for some advice. The warmth of the day feels good on my body. "Everything okay?" she answers right away.

"Yeah, why?"

"I just left your house and you're already calling."

I laugh at her observation, always so concerned for others. "I'm good. I just wanted to bounce something off you. Today is Logan's birthday."

"And?"

"He just left me a message inviting me to a barbecue tonight…"

"You should go."

"I know I should. But I don't think I can be around him," I tell her frustrated.

"Krane, he's your best friend. Clearly he cares about you. Go, have a few drinks, unwind, joke with Logan. You have the ability to make his night better. And if anyone asks you questions, just say you're there to focus on Logan, not you."

"I don't know if I'm up for it."

"Come on, loosen up, the way you do when we're together. It'll be good for both of you. I'll even drive you, if that helps."

"Ivy, that's sweet of you, but I can call a cab."

"So you're going?"

Damn, women are so good at getting me to do things sometimes. "Fine, I'll go, if you come with me. But you're driving, I might need some coercing to get out of the car."

"Okay, I'll go with you. What time should I pick you up?"

"Is five okay with you?"

"Perfect!"

We get off the phone and I know I need to

get measured for my tux or my sister is going to flip her shit entirely. Going through my messages, I find her texts and see a slew of new ones she sent me, panicking and pleading with me to do this for her. So I text her back, ***Going to get measured now!***

My sister means well. She just tries to juggle too much and because of that, like so many others, we have grown apart. It's more my fault than anything, but I don't give a shit about anyone anymore, not even myself.

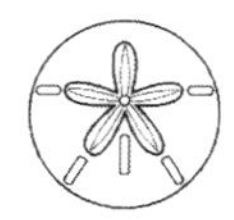

Knocking back another shot before I brush my teeth, the alcohol courses through my system and I'm thankful that Ivy is going to drive me. Her light knock on the door startles me, even though I knew she was coming. Jogging to the bathroom, I take a quick swig of mouthwash to hide the evidence of my drinking.

Opening the door, she takes my breath away. Her hair is down and messy – I've never seen it like this – and then my eyes scan her body and I shake away the inappropriate thoughts. "Come in," I tell her, leaning in and giving her a hug and soft kiss on the cheek. "You look good, really good," I say.

"Thanks, you too. It looks nice in here, you cleaned the place up?"

"Yeah, I had some time today; it was getting pretty gross."

She laughs and walks to the couch, my eyes following her ass tucked into a pair of skin tight shorts. Her flawless legs have me thinking what it would be like to fuck her. Running my hands over my face trying to scrub away the filth in my head, I tell her, "I just gotta do my hair, then we can go."

She sits on the couch and picks up Zoë's ring. I couldn't bear to do anything with it when I cleaned today, still regretting not leaving it with her when she was cremated. There are so many memories and pain that fill me when I even think about moving it.

Going into the bathroom, I splash some water on my face, and run it through my hair. Looking at my reflection in the mirror and the man I have become, I almost don't recognize myself anymore. The past has fucked me up, everything with Zoë broke me in half, and now I'm just lost, wasting away.

Wiping the tears from my eyes, I tell myself that I have to make a change, I have to try to move past all of this the best I can and somehow find the man that I am supposed to be. Because the man that I was died when Zoë took those last three breaths.

Walking back out to the living room, Ivy is fiddling with the ring and sets it back down on the coffee table. She looks at me like she's done something wrong, and I sit next to her, looking at the gold as it gleams in the light of the sun, the diamond sparkling like it did the day I gave it to Zoë.

"Will you take her ring for me?" I ask Ivy.

She looks at me, picking it back up and asks, "Why?"

"I can't have it here anymore. It's the smallest object in the room, but all I see."

"Why not put it away, or take it back to the apartment in the city?"

I give her half a laugh and get off the couch. Clearly, I'm worse off than she realizes. Looking down at her, I take a deep breath to clear my frustrations and keep my emotions in check. "I can't do any of that. I can't do anything without her." Tears fill my eyes and I turn away, I'm such a fucking pussy.

Walking into the kitchen, I grab the bottle of tequila, swallowing a huge mouthful. It burns badly, but it's not any worse than the pain that burns inside of me. Ivy comes behind me and wraps her arms around me. I look down at her hands and grab them. "I know it feels that way sometimes," she says against my back. "But it's not that way. Just take each moment as it comes and roll with it. That's what you have taught me to do and it helps."

I nod my head taking another swig of tequila. Ivy lets go of me and turns me towards her. I stare off, not able to bring my eyes to meet hers as they are filled with tears and I close them, so hurt and grief-stricken. However, I am caught off guard by her soft fingers as they cup my cheeks. I open my eyes and look at her. She gives me a small smile of encouragement and says, "Just breathe, Krane."

I let out a pent up puff of air and recalibrate my mind. I have to let Zoë go, she is not coming back, no matter what. I need to listen to Ivy and focus on each moment…because right now, that's all I have. It's all any of us have really, and I know better than anyone how that all can change.

"Thank you," I tell her placing my hands on her shoulders.

"Are you kidding me? You've done so much for me, Krane, and talked me off the ledge more times than I can even remember. It's the least I can do."

Kissing her on the forehead I pull her into a tight hug and set my chin on top of her head.

She smells so good. Dammit, Krane, get a grip.

"Are you ready?" I ask.

"Yeah, if you are."

Taking one of her hands in mine, I begin to head out. She holds on to me and I grab my keys and phone off the coffee table, noticing that Zoë's ring is gone. I'm so thankful to have Ivy around, for more ways than she'll ever know.

Chapter 8

Logan's wife, Victoria, passes he and I each a fresh brew. I take a pull and look down at my plate. This is really one of the only dinners that I have eaten and enjoyed in months. Ivy is picking at her fish fry and I can't help but give her a hard time. "Do you need help with that?"

She glares at me, and Logan whispers in my ear, "Are you two dating?"

I shake my head and he raises his eyebrows at me, laughing and knocking back a swallow of his drink. I look at Ivy, still struggling with her fish and grab her plate from her. She lets it go, and I take all of the fish off of the bone and then toss the carcass into the fire when I am done. Handing her back her plate, she responds sarcastically, "Thank you."

Logan looks between us and says, "Are you sure?"

"Yes," I snarl.

"Okay. So what's it going to take to get you back into the gym with me?"

"A fucking miracle," I respond, thankful that he has been cool tonight with not bringing up the past…until now.

"Come on, man, you said so yourself that you are still fighting. Even if it is underground, you need to work out so you don't get your ass whooped."

"I do my cardio. Right now, that's about all I can hold myself to. I haven't lost a fight yet."

He kicks the sand, rubbing his foot in a little deeper and asks, "Don't you want to really get back into it though and start contending for a belt? You're the most natural fighter I've ever seen."

I shake my head and toss my paper plate into the fire. "That was the old me, now I just want to make it through each day." I get off of the chair I'm sitting on and wander off. I know that Logan and everyone else here just wants what is best for me. But I don't give a shit about that stuff anymore.

Walking down to the water, I look out on the ocean. This isn't Long Beach, but I can still feel

Zoë with me. Her soul lives in the water. My heart hurts, feeling this close to her, yet so far away, and I rip my eyes off of the massive view. Walking aimlessly away from the noise, I chug my beer because my head can't take all of this anymore.

"Krane," I hear Ivy call from behind me. Looking back, she's jogging to me, and I smile seeing her.

"Sorry I left you," I tell her.

"It's all right, you good?"

"I guess," I respond and reach my hand out towards her. She looks down at the gesture before giving her hand over to me. With her hand tightly in my hold, we begin to walk along the beach. I'm not sure what my plan is, or what we are doing, but all I know is that it feels really good to have her by my side.

Looking ahead, I catch sight of something white being washed up on shore. We approach it just as it's about to get sucked out to sea again. "What's that?" Ivy asks as I pull it up from the water.

I hand her the perfectly round sand dollar and she stares at it like I just gave her a stack of cash. "You never find these intact and so…perfect," she says.

"Must be your lucky day." My phone rings as she looks at me with the most incredible eyes, so clear and beautiful.

Pulling my phone out, I hesitate answering when I see it's Ling. I don't want this night to end, but I can't let the call go.

"What up, Ling?"

"Krane, do I have an opportunity for you tonight, my man."

"What's that?" I ask.

"A fight in the Bronx against none other than the Resolution."

I can see now why he gave me all the details up front, knowing that I haven't given two shits in the past about who I fight. But the Resolution was blacklisted from professional fighting for using HGH almost a year ago, so he's no fucking joke. I think about the offer. Normally I'd jump all over a fight, I need the money, but fighting anywhere in the state of New York is illegal. All of my fights typically take place in Jersey or Boston. "I don't know, man, I'm not sure it's worth it."

"Come on, it'll be safe. I've got the perfect place set up, with some of New York's finest on my payroll to keep an eye out. I'll even double your normal pay, and let's say if you win I'll give you an extra G."

"What time?"

"Eight. Should I text you the address?"

"Yeah."

I hang up, and look at Ivy. There is worry in her eyes. "A fight?" she asks, knowing me so fucking well.

Facing her, I nod. "Thank you for everything today. I'm sorry to cut things short tonight, but I need the money."

"Don't be sorry. I understand. I can come with you, if you want. You probably shouldn't be driving."

"No, you don't have to, I'll take a cab."

She cups my cheek and I lean into her touch; her warmth feels so right. "I want to." I close my eyes and know that I want her there with me tonight, too.

"You sure?" I ask.

She nods her head and I grab the back of her head, kissing her forehead. A text comes through my phone from Ling with the address and I check the time, "We need to get going."

She pulls her keys from her back pocket and

says, "I'm ready."

I text Logan, ***Happy birthday brother, sorry, I got called for a fight. Love ya, buddy.***

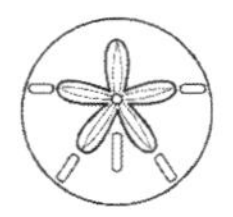

"I think this is the place," I tell Ivy as she puts her car in park. We both look up at the brick building and then I ask her, "Are you ready?"

She nods her head and we proceed. Being back in the city feels different than I imagined. I thought when I came back here it was going to be harder than it is right now. But my insides are coursing with adrenaline. I need to fight badly.

We walk down the alley where Ling's usual guy is watching the back door, and I notice a NYPD cop car parked on the other side – that's what Ling must've meant about them being on his payroll.

"Where am I heading?" I ask one of Ling's guys.

"Down the stairs and to the left."

I grab Ivy's hand as we enter and suddenly worry bringing her here was wrong – there's no one to protect her while I fight and these guys get rowdy. As we walk down the stairs, I look for Ling or Bo, but neither is in sight. The safest bet is to get into the room and one of them will be in to check on things soon.

The crowd is cheering and Ivy says, "God, it's loud."

"These guys have a lot of money riding on these fights. I'll get someone to watch out for you while I do my thing."

She squeezes my hand and we enter the room that has my name on it. This place is much cleaner than the room where I normally get ready. Thank God, or Ivy might have reconsidered coming.

Unzipping my bag, I pull out what I need and look for a bathroom. Of course there isn't one in here. I guess cleaner isn't always better. Looking at Ivy with my stuff in my hand I say, "Wanna turn around?"

She smiles and turns her back to me, "I've already seen what you work with," she chuckles getting out her cell phone to keep busy while I change. I turn away too and as I adjust my junk under the cup, my cock is starting to grow.

What the fuck? Not now.

I close my eyes trying to think of anything else, but her sitting in here with me while I'm basically naked is making me hard. I pull my shorts up and turn around to catch her looking over her shoulder at me. "Were you staring at my ass again?" I ask.

"No way. I was just…stretching my neck." And she turns her head in the other direction.

I smirk at her lie and sit on the bench next to her, pulling my tape from my bag. Placing a strip over my knuckles first, I begin to wrap them.

"Is that all you use to protect them?"

"Fights like this, yeah. The way I used to fight, we'd have thin gloves over our knuckles." There is a knock on the door and Ling pops his head in.

"Hey, man, you ready for this?"

"You know it."

Ling looks at Ivy and I introduce her to him. "This is my friend, Ivy. Ivy, this is Ling; he puts these fights together."

"It's nice to meet you," she says and they shake hands.

"Likewise. You're up in five, you need anything?"

"Nah, man, nothing for me. But I was wondering if you could have Bo watch over Ivy? I know the crowd gets pretty crazy."

"Yeah, for sure, I'll get him now."

Ling leaves and I look Ivy in the eyes. My heart is pounding against the walls of my chest and not because I'm nervous to fight, but because I'm worried that something is going to happen to her.

"You ready?" she asks.

I nod my head and sling an arm over her shoulder. She hugs me back and as we sit here in one another's hold, I breathe her in, her scent so familiar, yet so new.

"You can stay in here, if you'd rather?" I ask her.

"No way, I wanna see you fight."

I nod my head once and kiss her forehead, she holds me back tightly and I get up to stretch, knowing I don't have much time. Suddenly, Bo opens the boor. "You're up first," he says and I look at him confused.

"Why?"

"Not sure, it was Ling's call."

Asshole!

I keep calm externally, because with Ivy here, I don't want to start shit with any of these guys.

"My grand bonus is yours Bo if you keep her very safe." Grabbing her hand, I lead her out of the room. The crowd chants my name, which gets my blood boiling. Letting go of Ivy, I get myself hyped up as we round the corner and the enormous arena that this is all taking place in. "Don't take your eyes off of her," I tell Bo.

"For sure, man. Get after it!"

Walking out, the room erupts when I enter. The sound of stomping on the metal risers echoes and it brings me into my zone. I don't give a fuck who's in front of me. I haven't lost a fight in years, so I sure as hell am not going to start now, especially with Ivy here.

Looking back at Ivy as the ref checks me before I enter the cage, she looks happy. I wink at her and run up the stairs, doing some sprints across to get my blood flowing, then jump up and down as the Resolution makes his entrance. He's about the same size as I am, maybe a little taller and he's looking right at me.

I keep my eyes locked, eager and ready…

Then the bell dings and we size each other up. Boxing back and forth. He's got a strong jaw. My hits don't seem to do much to him, although he is slower than I am. We work each other like this for a few minutes and the crowd starts to get restless, booing.

I worry for Ivy being stuck in the middle of it and look to see her watching me safely with Bo by her side, but my attention being diverted costs me a mistake and I'm caught with a right hook. Knowing that I can't hang with his boxing all night, I take him to the ground, but he works his way on top of me.

Lying underneath him, I try and block the hits that continue to connect with my face. Ivy's screams are loud, then the bell rings and the round ends. Getting off of the floor, I spit a mouthful of blood at the Resolution as he walks away from me. Being taken to the ground and not having the advantage is not what I do. One of Ling's guys sits me down and tries to clean me up, but I push him away. Only looking at my opponent before the next round gets the fire going inside of me.

He looks at me and winks, like the cocky bastard that he is. With my chest heaving up and down, I stand waiting to annihilate him. Round two begins and with every ounce of strength inside me, I launch a back kick. Spinning hard and high, landing it on the side of his head, everything happens in slow motion. His head drops, shoulders slump, and his body falls to the ground like a ton of bricks. My signature move worked.

Quickly, I get on top of him to do as much damage as I can, before the ref calls the fight, but the kick knocked him out cold so before I can enjoy a few more hits, the ref pulls me away. Getting to my feet, I look at Ivy as my hand is held high in the air. She is jumping up and down screaming.

Walking out of the cage, she runs to me and hugs me hard. With her in my arms, it takes me back to when Zoë would be so excited for me after a fight. She'd have that same look on her face. But knowing that Zoë can't share in this victory resonates inside of me. I squeeze Ivy back, kissing the top of her soft brown hair. Zoë might not be here in person, but she was shining down on me for this one.

Chapter 9

Moving my body to adjust myself a little, I am sore as fuck. As I open my eyes, I look at the ceiling and bring in the room. I'm on my couch, like usual, but I'm sitting up. The tightness of my skin tells me my face is fucked up.

Fuck, I gotta piss.

I attempt to get up, but I am stopped dead in my tracks. Ivy is sleeping peacefully on my lap. She is still wearing her clothes from yesterday and I rack my brain to remind myself of what happened to wake up like this. I remember the fight, and then she brought me home, and we must've fallen asleep talking, 'cause that's the last thing I remember.

Looking down at her lying so beautifully, I can't help but touch her face, running the backs of my knuckles down her cheek. We've both been through so much, and it makes me happy to see her at peace like this. She stirs a little, so I stop touching her, fearing that I will wake her up, and sure enough, it does. Her tired eyes open so innocently.

"Hey," I say to her with a smile on my face.

"Morning. What time is it?" she asks.

"Not sure, it's light out though."

She blinks a few times and looks out my balcony window. However, she is not quick to sit up. I don't know what is going on between the two of us, but I'm enjoying being around her right now. She looks up at me again and says, "Oh God, Krane, we really need to get some ice on your face."

"Nah, I'll be fine. But I do have to piss, if you'd let me up."

"Yeah, sorry," she says and suddenly sits up.

"Don't be." I take my thumb and forefinger to her chin, bringing her eyes to meet mine. She looks at me with uncertainty and I run my thumb over her bottom lip, before walking off and into the bathroom.

Christ, my face is really fucked up.

Staring at my reflection in the mirror, anger boils inside of me. There is no reason that I should've let this happen. Had I listened to my gut and taken the Resolution to the ground right off the bat, I could've ended things with him landing just a few hits on me. But I also have to admit it was Ivy's pull on me last night that got my face into this situation. *What the fuck is up with me?* "I'm gonna shower," I yell out to Ivy, "Feel free to make some coffee if you want."

"Okay."

Turning the water on, I shed my clothes and then get right in. The water is only lukewarm and it sends a shiver down my spine. Quickly it heats up and once it's hot, I hold my breath sticking my face underneath it. I let it burn every cut and abrasion so it can wash away all the dried blood and maybe clear my swirling mind. Resting my hands on the wall in front of me, I tilt my head down and take a deep breath. The water running down the drain is pink. I wait for it to be clear and know then that at least the stinging will stop, even if my head can't get right.

"Krane?" Ivy calls out knocking on the door.

"Yeah."

"Can I come in and pee?"

I smile to myself, imagining her in here with me, then push the thoughts away. "Of course."

"Thanks," she says now more clearly, her

voice is no longer muffled as if she's in the hall.

"Sorry, I forgot to ask you if you needed to go."

"It's okay." Then she is silent and I grab the soap, wondering if she'll say anything else. I begin to wash myself and it stays silent. There are no noises at all and I ask her, "Stage fright?"

"A little, can you talk or something so it's not so quiet."

I chuckle at her comment, "You know, Ivy, everyone pisses and everyone—"

"All right, all right," she cuts me off. "I know what everyone does, but I've never gone with a guy in the room."

I stick my head around the shower curtain, with my eyes wide, not really able to believe her. "Are you kidding me?"

"Krane!" she scolds me.

"Sorry." I go back to my shower, but the image of her sitting so properly with her shorts barely pulled down, stays comfortably in my mind. The room is yet again silent, so I decide to sing to help her along. She giggles at my horrible voice and very bad rendition, but it works. I hear the toilet flush just as I'm finished with my shower.

Drying off, I look over my face and the damage that was done. It'll be bad for Mia's wedding, but there really isn't a thing that I can do about it now.

I get dressed in a pair of sweatpants and find Ivy lost in my kitchen as I head to the laundry room, looking for a t-shirt. "Where are the coffee filters?" she asks.

I pull open the drawer they are in. "Don't ask me why I keep them in here, I just do." She laughs as I hand her one and I notice her staring at my body. I smirk and kiss her on the forehead before continuing into the laundry room.

"Do you want me to make some eggs or something?" she asks.

"Fuck yeah, girl," I reply and pull a thin white t-shirt over my head.

"Here, keep this on your face," she tosses me an ice pack. "I think the hot water from your shower made the swelling worse." I press the ice to the right side of my face, where most of the damage is and realize how much Ivy has sacrificed for me.

She's always there, pulling my ass out of the fucked up rut that is my life, and then when I need her advice, she not only gives it to me, but she spends the day and night with me, getting me reconnected to friends, and going above and beyond to show she's in my corner.

Watching her in the kitchen, I realize that when I'm around her, all the bad shit from the past sort of vanishes. All of my thoughts and pain are so much less, making my life somewhat tolerable. "Thank you for everything, especially for yesterday, it was nice to have you at the fight."

"It was good to be there," she tells me, pushing her hair behind her ear.

My phone rings, interrupting us. I find it charged on the counter behind me and I know Ivy plugged it in. My sister's calling. "Good morning, Mia," I answer.

"Whoa, you sound chipper today."

"That's nice of you to say, but really I'm just extremely happy you called," I tease her.

"Spare me, Krane. I know you better than that."

"Fine, you got me," I say in a little more somber tone.

"There's my baby brother."

"What the fuck can you need this early in the morning?" I ask. She's agitating me already.

"Well, you haven't booked your room for the wedding this weekend and I was wondering where you were planning on staying?"

"I was gonna stay in yours, isn't that cool with you?"

"Ha," she laughs out loud. "The fuck you will. I'm going to book a room for you. It'll be my present to you for being the best man. Although I'm still not sure why Wayne picked you since you haven't done shit for him."

"What was that?" I ask, now pissed off at her.

"Nothing, I'll email you the details."

"You do that, Mia." I hang up annoyed by her comment and toss my phone aside.

"She piss you off?" Ivy asks me.

"Yup, her wedding is this weekend and she's just calling to bust my balls, being stupid as always. Fucking women sometimes, you know?"

"Hey," Ivy exclaims.

"Damn, I'm sorry."

She glares at me opening the cabinet. "Plates?" she asks.

I open another drawer and hand her a few paper ones. "Why do you keep everything in drawers?"

"I don't know, I just throw shit where it'll fit." She serves our eggs and I pour us each a cup of coffee. She adds sugar to hers and I drink mine black.

"Wanna eat outside?"

"Yeah, I'd like that."

We take our food out to the patio and sit down looking at each other for a brief moment. Ivy has an uncertain look in her eye and then asks me, "What are we doing here, Krane?"

Taking a bite I respond, "Uhh, eating."

"I know that! I mean with us?"

I look her in the eye, contemplating how to answer her. *Why is she doing this right now?* Cocking my head to the side as I speak, I do my best to stay calm. "Ivy, you mean a lot to me, probably more than you realize, but I don't know how to answer your question. Most of the time I don't know what the fuck I'm doing. If what I'm giving you right now isn't enough, I'm really sorry, but each breath is still a struggle for *me*."

"And you think it's not for me?"

"I know it is. I'm trying here, Ivy."

"Are you?" she jibes back.

I glare at her, caught off guard by her sudden animosity. "Of course I am."

"Sometimes, it doesn't feel like it anymore," she says with tears in her eyes.

"Why would you say that? I think things have been great." I hate to see her upset like this.

"I don't know, lately things feel different. That's why I wanted to know what we we're doing."

"I told you, eating."

"This isn't a fucking joke, Krane. You can't even answer a simple question."

"Ivy, you're running with expectations for us, and I'm not sure why. I mean, I didn't ask you to drive me to Logan's party, or to my fight, or to stay the night with me last night. That was all you."

She blinks a few times, obviously hurt by my words and sets her fork down.

Fuck!

"I'm sorry," I say, trying to repair some of the damage.

She gets up from the table with tears in her eyes and says, "I gotta get going." The thought of her leaving panics me and I grab her hand, trying to make this right. "I didn't mean for it to come out like that. I enjoy being around you, I really do. You keep my mind busy, but to have expectations on things right now, that's just not something I can handle."

"Clearly, we have different feelings on things."

A stray tear rolls down her cheek and I watch it fall, speechless. I need to make this right, but something inside won't let me. She's more than likely better off without me, just like everyone else is. I mean, I can't even be a good friend to her, or take things serious when I need to. I don't make her a better person, I only bring her down and that's because I'm fucking miserable. It's the last thing that I want to do, especially to her.

She can pull out of this, I know she can and she will…but I can't.

As I come back from my internal mindfuck, she's gone. I run my hands through my hair, wondering where did it all go so wrong?

Chapter 10

Sitting alone and sober for the first time in a week, I'm lost. I haven't talked to Ivy. I know I hurt her, she won't respond to my texts or calls, which I can't blame her. However, with Mia's wedding imminent, I wish now more than ever that I had Ivy to lean on.

The dryer buzzes and I grab the last few clothing items I need before I hit the road. Taking my phone and charger, I see a text from my sister. *Will you make sure that you clean yourself up before the wedding?*

What the fuck does that mean? Placing my phone into my pocket, I walk to the bathroom and look at my worn-out reflection in the mirror. My hair is long and shaggy, way overdue for a haircut, which Zoë used to cut for me. And my face is still fucked up from the fight, all scabbed and bruised. If I show up to the wedding looking like this, my entire family will have a fucking fit. So I grab the clippers from under the sink and plug them in. They buzz and vibrate in my hand. As I look down at them, I can still picture Zoë holding them when she would meticulously cut my hair. Fuck, sometimes it hurts to do the simplest of things.

After I lost Zoë, my parents went to our apartment to get my clothes and some essentials, and these clippers were one of the things they brought me. I'm not sure why; I didn't ask for them. But right now, I'm grateful. Placing the cold steel at the base of my head, I lift upward and continue forward, shaving off all of my hair. I'm not even sure what guard is on here or what the adjustment is set to, but if Mia wants me cleaned up, well, then here you fucking go.

I repeat the motions again and again and then run my hands over my cleanly shaven head. Staring back at myself a little disconcerted, I'm so confused with the man that I've become. I've slipped so far away from who I used to be.

Brushing off the extra hair with a towel, I need to hit the road – the faster I get there, the sooner I can drink. I grab my bag and get in my truck to head towards the Hamptons, a place I sure as hell won't fit in.

After an hour and a half of driving, I'm starving and anxious. Pulling up to the lavish hotel that Mia booked, I look for somewhere to park. Not seeing one spot, I decide to valet, then head inside keeping my sunglasses on, knowing the more I can hide the marks on my face, the better.

Walking in, I spot the check-in counter, and hear my name from behind me before I make it there. "Krane," my mom calls out again. Slowly, I turn to see her, my dad, Mia, Wayne, and Shannon, Mia's friend and I think the maid of honor, all staring at me. As much as I don't want to, I know I have to remove my sunglasses and their expressions say it all. Both my mother and Mia gasp.

"What in God's name happened to you?" my dad asks.

"I had a rough fight."

"Oh my God, Krane," Mia whines, "Do you realize how many pictures you are going to be in?"

"And your hair," my mom adds. "What did you do?"

"Mia asked me to clean up, so I did. You all know what I do for a living, so my face shouldn't be a surprise." Everyone seems to be horrified by my appearance, except for Shannon…she just looks like she wants to jump me. I'm not sure why some girls are turned on by guys who fight, but whatever.

Mia storms off, like the drama queen that she is. Wayne and Shannon follow her and my dad says, "I didn't think you were back into fighting."

"Well, I am. How do you think I've been paying my bills and for two apartments?"

My mom steps to me and cups my cheek, "You should see a doctor. This looks infected." She looks intently at a cut under my eye and I brush her hand away.

"I'm fine, Mom, really I am." She shakes her head at my response and looks around the lobby. I was a little loud in my reaction and clearly she's not wanting to bring any more attention than the eyes that are already staring at us. "I'm gonna check in, I'll see you later."

"Here's your key," my dad says passing me a small card. "It's room one ten."

I take it from him and walk off, leaving him and my mom, because quite frankly I need to get away. Being here alone is already harder than I expected it to be. If I had Zoë or even Ivy right now, I'd be handling this all differently. But, since they are both gone, I'm fucking angry and lost.

Not having Ivy this week to depend on the way that I had been has been hard. She got me through so much these last six months and now all because I can't open up to her and give her more, I've lost her. Opening the door to the ridiculously elegant room, I set my bag on the bed and laugh to myself. My sister is truly a piece of work, booking a room like this and not thinking twice about spending the money on it. As I take out the handle of tequila that I brought with me, I count on the next few drinks to ease the pain. Pouring myself a massive glass, I swallow a huge mouthful and lie back on the bed.

Thinking about how my parents and Mia reacted has me stressed to go through all of this shit. Pulling out my phone, I dial Ivy. I need to talk to her and hope she'll answer. But my call goes straight to voicemail and I hang up, pissed off.

Then there is a knock on my door and I contemplate not answering it, but knowing my crazy ass family, there's no other option. Getting up, I open the door to find Wayne staring at me. I step aside and gesture him in. He looks at the drink in my hand and I say, "If you came here to give me a fucking lecture, save it, man."

He sits in one of the chairs in the corner of the room and shakes his head. "You know that's not why I'm here. You have to understand your sister. She's really happy that you're here, she's just stressed."

"Aren't we all?" I respond under my breath.

"She has this vision that the wedding needs to be perfect, man, and I keep telling her it's not going to be, that nothing's perfect, but you know how women are; cut her a little slack."

I take in his words, not really buying the bull-shit that he's selling. Stressed or not, Mia needs to let the fuck up and lay off my balls. "Wanna drink?" I ask, refilling mine.

"Sure." I hand him a glass and sit in the other chair waiting for what else he has to say. I know Wayne, he didn't just come here to tell me that Mia is happy that I'm here and to give her a break.

"Krane, I lost a girlfriend in college." He pauses staring at the carpet and as I watch him, I can see the pain contorting his face.

"You did?" I ask, shocked by his confession.

"Yeah, she was my first love," he says, with a wide smile remembering her. "We had so many plans for the future and then one night she overdosed. We were partying and I found her in the bathroom. What I'm trying to say is I've been where you are, brother. I don't even remember the year after she died, I was a fuckin' zombie. So I get what you're going through, and I know everything feels hopeless and not worth it, but it *will* get better, and one day you will move on. When I found your sister, it was when I least expected it, and she pulled me from the darkness that I lived in. I didn't think I would ever love again and because of her, I do. I know she's hard on you, but it's because she loves you and wants what's best for you. Family isn't perfect, man, you know that, but give her and your parents a little slack sometimes."

I finish my drink with tears in my eyes, like a pussy. His words take me back to the night that I lost Zoë – she was my world, my everything. "I don't know how to be without her. I'm so lost and angry inside."

"You gotta let the anger go, for Zoë, and just be yourself."

"I've been trying to, but the man I've become is not good enough for anyone, especially my parents and Mia. They all keep riding me like I'm not making them happy. No matter what I do, it isn't good enough."

"You know what, Krane? You have to be true to yourself right now. There's no one else who's gonna look out for you, except you. Try and find the person you are meant to be right now." Wayne's phone rings and he looks at it. "It's Mia; we have the rehearsal at three."

I nod and watch Wayne answer it. "Hey, baby," he says and right away, I can hear my sister upset through the phone. He takes it away from his ear and says to me, "I'm gonna get going. Text me if you need to talk, brother." I nod and listen to him calm my sister down as he leaves my room. I never would have thought that he'd experienced something so similar.

Wayne's always had his shit together. He's actually been someone that I've looked up to. It's why we've connected. But seeing the pain in his eyes as he talked about the girl he lost shows me that no matter how much time passes, it never really gets any better. Losing the one person you love most will hurt you and haunt you for years. Yeah, he might have moved on with Mia, but the smile that was on his face as he remembered the past was nothing I've ever seen from him. I've had that smile myself and I'm convinced I'll never have it again.

Chapter 11

"To Mia and Wayne," I force myself to announce. The alcohol flows through my system, boosting me on a high that will get me through the next few hours.

The room erupts in cheers and I've done my deed for the weekend. I've been fake as fuck, which is what my sister needed me to do, and now...I'm fucking done. Walking outside, the Atlantic Ocean shines in the moonlight. The waves splash against the shore, making my unsteady feet feel grounded as I watch their rhythmic motion. God, I love this feeling, so blitzed out of my mind that nothing else matters.

Not Zoë, not Ivy, nothing. Fuck life. I'm fucking numb to it all.

Walking down to a desolate spot, I get close enough to feel the ocean mist and then plop down, pushing my beer into the sand. As I lie back, I look up at the stars and watch the sky morph, twisting from the alcohol coursing through my veins. I close my eyes focusing on what's inside of me.

I laugh sadistically to myself.

I feel nothing.

Everything that I used to be is fucking gone now.

I'm empty.

There wasn't much before anyways, only agony and regret. The agony over the loss of Zoë and the regret over not being able to be a good friend to Ivy. I'm fucked up. But cutting ties with her is what needed to be done. I'm no good for her. I'll only hurt her in the long run and she deserves someone so much better.

Someone that can give her the world.

Sitting up, I finish the last of my beer and rest back on my elbows, letting out a deep breath. My phone rings and I struggle to pull it from my pocket. I answer it without even looking at the screen, "What's up?" I ask and wait, but don't hear anyone on the other end.

"Yes, is Samantha there?" an older gentleman asks.

"You have the wrong fucking number," I yell

and hang up. Looking at the screen, it's a number I don't recognize. But as I stare at the call log for the last few days, it shows I have called Ivy over a dozen times. And I've texted her at least double that.

I'm so pathetic!

She hasn't responded once, and I guess I should try to respect the boundary she's obviously trying to draw.

Fuck me.

Going into my contacts, I delete her number. It's the only way I can be sure I'll stop harassing her.

Clearly, she wants nothing to do with me and maybe it's for the best. Once the number is gone, I delete the call log and texts and then take the last of my beer in one gulp.

Getting off the sand, I head back into the hotel and to the bar where Shannon is sitting and ask her, "Is this seat taken?" She looks at me with her tight black dress distracting me and responds, "Nope."

I sit down and notice her glass is almost empty. "What are you drinking?"

"Merlot."

"Can she get another Merlot?" I ask the bartender, getting his attention as he's talking to another employee.

He fills her glass and I pass my empty beer to him. He hands me a full one and she's got a huge smile on her face. "Thanks, I've been trying to get his attention for like ten minutes."

"Of course." I take a swig and sense she's staring at me. Like she's been all weekend. Looking over at her, she's leaning on the bar basically resting her tits on it and I'm not sure what to say next.

"How are you doing, Krane?" she asks.

"Good, when I'm drunk."

"Amen to that," she says taking a drink. "Isn't there something that can make you happy though? You're back into fighting I hear."

"Only for the money really."

"You know, I'm a nurse, I can clean your face up if you'd let me."

"Nah, I'm good," I respond.

"Really?" She leans over and whispers in my ear, "You'd be missing out." She's a little obvious in her attempt to hit on me, but for some reason I like it. Pulling away from her, I pat the stool next to me and she slides over to it. I lean into her ear and ask, "Tell me what I'd be missing out on?"

My eyes scan her tight body tucked into her little dress and she takes a huge drink of wine resting her elbow on the bar. She runs her tongue over her lips and says, "Well, my lips for starters, I'd love to wrap them around your dick."

My cock grows instantly, awakening my body from her words. "Can I come deep in your throat?"

She nods her head and right away I grab her hand, feeling unsteady, but not caring. Leading her away from the bar and towards my room. As I look over at her soft red lips, my cock is throbbing. I open the door to my room and usher her inside. She takes her black high heels off and watches me remove my bowtie, then steps to me and deftly unbuttons my shirt. I stand there and let her do with me what she wants, bracing my weight on the wall next to me.

With only my pants on, I reach down and grab a handful of one of her tits. I'm spinning as she moans from my touch, pushing me backwards. I flop on top of the plush bed and watch her push the arms of her dress down, and then slowly she glides it down the rest of her body.

She has no bra on and as I lean up on my

elbows, she removes her panties.

Jesus, I want to fuck her.

I lean back as she kneels on the bed next to me and rubs my cock through my pants, waiting for her next move. Her touch feels so good that long blinks take over as I enjoy this.

"Touch me," she instructs, and I open my eyes, cupping her sex. She unzips my pants freeing my dick. She takes ahold of me and I reach her pussy, working two of my fingers in. She's wet and I take the opportunity to penetrate her. She gasps, pushing down on me and grinds herself against my hand.

She's horny and I love it.

Knowing she likes this, I finger her hard and fast. She gets lost in the moment, gripping my dick. "Suck me," I command her. She falls forward, lips first, and takes my cock into her mouth.

I push my hips up, giving her a little more of my length, and we both work each other. Me with my fingers tucked tightly inside of her cunt, and her leaning down with my cock rubbing the back of her throat. My balls are tight and pleasure radiates through my body.

She sucks me good, making everything inside

so hot. I want to fuck her badly as my balls begin to erupt and she moans, causing me to come harder. Letting go with my eyes closed, I fill her mouth with my cum.

For a very brief moment, I forget about all of the bad shit from the past and find a peace that lives deep inside of me.

However, quickly it ends and as I open my eyes, I'm determined to get it back. Pulling my cock away from her, I ask her, "Do you have a condom?" She reaches into her purse and hands me one. I waste no time tearing it open and rolling it down my hard shaft.

"Fuck me!" Then I guide her on top of me. She blinks a few times breathing heavily and whining as I work my way inside of her. I reach for her clit, rubbing it with my thumb as she watches me and then tosses her head back. I stroke myself inside of her. The walls of her pussy are so warm as she engulfs me.

Holding on to her sides, I help guide her up and down as I move my hips along with her. She braces her weight on my chest and bobs up and down. "Fuck, yes," she cries out loud.

"You like fucking me, don't you?" I grunt. The satisfaction of her on top of me and my cock pleasing her has me feeling great. I enjoy pumping her pussy. Her long black hair touches my thighs as her head hangs back.

"Fuck me," she begs.

"Like this?" I ask, slamming our bodies together.

"Harder!" she demands.

I push her off of me and hold her facedown on the bed. Even being blitzed out of my mind, I stay in control. Reaching down I grip myself and slam into her from behind. She screams and says, "Yes, like that!"

"Take my cock!" I slam into her again and again.

"Yes!" she chants.

Her skin is red and I rest my hand on the small of her back as I pummel her. "Oh, God, Krane, make me com—" her words change to a scream and she shakes violently underneath me.

"That's it, come on my dick," I growl.

Her body settles and I pull out of her, lifting her ass up so she is lined up with me perfectly. Running my forearm over my forehead, I wipe away the sheen of sweat and jolt myself into her. Leaning forward, I pump at a good pace getting lost in the sensation before I blow another load of cum, grunting barbarically, owning this pleasure…again.

Chapter 12

Waking up next to Shannon, she is wrapped in my arms, her hot body still naked and I wonder how in the world we ended up together last night. My head is pounding and my brain feels mushy. I close my eyes, recalling the events that took place and all I can remember is pounding her over and over again.

Man, she was a good fuck, and a good distraction.

Looking back down at her and those lips, I can picture them wrapped so tightly around my dick. I'd love to come from them again. "Morning," she says, slowly blinking her eyes.

"Good morning."

She rolls over and looks at the clock, "Oh fuck."

Then her phone rings and she jumps out of bed, scurrying around trying to find her purse. I can't help but laugh. "What's the hurry?" The wedding is over, so I see no reason to rush. I'd rather her stay and fuck me again, but she pulls on her underwear and says, "I'm an hour late for work."

I'm silent as she pulls her dress over her head and tames her hair in the mirror, looking at me in the reflection. "Thank you for last night."

I wink and then she scoops her shoes and purse off of the floor. But before I can answer her, she's gone. I'm a little baffled by what just happened. But with how I am right now, it's better that she's gone; she was a good distraction and lay, but that's it. Getting up, I shower to wash away last night's remnants. Letting the water run over me, I can't help but think of Ivy as I stare at the inside of the shower curtain and remember not so long ago when she sat on the other side. Even though I've pushed her as far out of my mind as possible, I'll never forget her.

Sliding on a pair of underwear, I walk out of the bathroom and am startled by my mom gathering my tux off the floor.

"What's going on, Mom?"

"Hey, Krane, sorry to barge in, but your dad kept the extra key."

Of course he did.

Thank God she didn't walk in last night.

"I was just collecting your tux; I'm gonna return it for you when we get back home."

"Thanks, Mom. I think I left my coat at the bar last night."

"I'll find it for you, dear." She looks at me with the ball of my clothes tightly in her grip. "Thank you for everything that you did for Mia this weekend." She goes to leave and I stop her.

"Mom."

"Yes, Krane."

"Thank you for putting up with me. I know I'm difficult."

"It's my job, you're my only son. I'm worried for you. I only want what's best for you, and sometimes I don't know how to help you with that, but I won't give up. I'm always here if you ever want to talk."

I'd rather not burden my mom with my problems. Kissing her on the cheek, I close the door behind her, praying my apology will cover my shitty behavior these last several months. The look in her eyes was hopeful, a great thing to see, but it won't last long. I'll let her down again; I always do.

Packing up my bag, I see a missed call from

an unknown number. There is a message and as I play it on speaker, my world yet again…crumbles down around me.

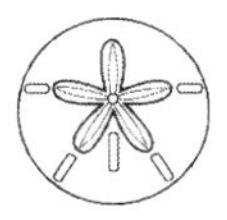

"What do you mean I have 'til the end of the month?" I ask the overly rude woman on the other end of the line.

"I'm sorry, Mr. Hensley, but you and Miss Winslow only signed a one-year lease. I'm afraid that this is your last month and with the current economy, rates have gone up. I can look and see if we have a cheaper apartment for you to move into."

"Didn't you hear what I said? Zoë's dead and I don't even live there anymore."

"Then what's the problem with moving out?"

I hang up on her. I'm not about to get more into my personal life than I already have. I've known for a while that this was coming; now I'm just forced to actually do it. This falls on my shoulders. Zoë was mine, she was my fiancée and soon would have been my wife, so I have to handle her things.

But imagining doing it without Ivy is almost impossible. Looking through my contacts, I panic needing to talk to her. And then remember what I did last night. Fuck, I really wish I hadn't deleted her number. Looking out the window, resolve settles over me.

I have to go see her to make things right and it isn't 'cause I need her right now. It's because as I think of the things I did last night, I'm more and more convinced that is not the person I want to be. Ivy makes me better, and a week without her has broken me even further down than six months without Zoë already has. I'm drinking even more now. I miss my friend, plain and simple. I don't want anything more than to see her smile and be there for each other like we used to be.

Jogging down the stairs of my apartment, I get in my truck and check the time. She should still be working, so I head that way hoping I don't piss her off showing up there.

Parking in the first spot I see, I head inside on a mission. As I look around wildly for her, I am disappointed when I don't spot her, so I tell the receptionist, "I'm here to see Ivy Winslow, please."

She blinks a few times and then says, "I'm sorry, but she doesn't work here anymore."

"What?" I ask the girl, confused.

"She's no longer employed here." The woman repeats slowly, like I am a fucking idiot.

"Since when?" I ask, agitated, gripping the counter.

"I don't have the authority to—"

I cut her off, pissed, and lean lower, getting in her face. "Since when?" I ask again, in a low, deep voice.

She looks around the room, and then whispers, "Since last week. She just stopped coming in is all I know."

I shake my head, sick with fear, and pat the counter once before I walk off. Why in the world would she stop going in to work? Driving to her apartment as quickly as I can, I weave in and out of traffic, fearing that this is all my fault.

Parking at her house, I see her car parked in her normal spot as I shut mine off.

She better fucking be okay.

Sprinting up to the door, I knock and wait. It's quiet inside and I feel like something is off. "Ivy," I shout and bang again, but there is no response.

Fuck!

Looking at my phone, I try and rack my brain to remember her phone number, but can't. "Ivy?" I shout and slam my fist again, but she doesn't come to the door. As I start to panic, I try and rationalize with myself as to what could have actually happened. But alarm bells ring in my head; if she stopped going to work a week ago, something's wrong. Reaching for the door handle, I turn it and find it unlocked.

Goddammit, my heart stammers.

My mind is swirling with a million different scenarios, all of them flash to the image of Zoë as the cops pulled me away from her.

"Ivy," I call out stepping into her dark apartment, closing the door behind me.

The place is trashed. Her cat jumps on the counter and meows at me. I scratch his head as I walk by, looking at the wreckage. Someone ransacked the place. The shelves of all of her things are empty. The floor is littered with debris, and she is nowhere in sight. So I head towards her bedroom and hesitantly place my hand on the door handle.

Slowly, I open the door afraid of what I

might find, and there she is in her bed. My eyes move to her chest, and when I catch it moving, slow steady breaths rolling through her, I can breathe again as it's apparent she's asleep. Tears fill my eyes and I drop my hand from the knob that has been holding me up before I walk to her bed. Taking in the sights of the room as I sit next to her, I find the sand dollar I gave her placed on the center of her nightstand. I take one of my hands and gently move the hair out of her face.

Christ, she's gorgeous when she sleeps.

She moves a little and when I lock my eyes on her lips, I can't help but run my thumb over them. Being in the same room with her again makes everything in my world okay. The pain lessens and everything is a little bit more tolerable. The agony that normally eats away at my insides has settled.

Leaning down, I press my lips to her forehead, breathing her in. She's so special to me. She and Zoë are so different. Ivy is her own person, so beautiful and unique.

Pulling away, I'm not sure what to do next and notice she is looking right at me. I wipe away my tears, not wanting to look like a pussy for crying and say, "Hey."

"Hi," she quietly responds and a flood of tears pool in her eyes.

"No, don't cry, Ivy."

She reaches for me and I kick my shoes off, lying next to her, wrapping one arm under her pillow and with the other I hold on to her cheek, wiping away her tears. She cries harder and I pull her into my chest, knotting my fingers into the back of her hair. Her body rocks as she sobs and I just hold on to her, letting her be.

Running my hand over the back of her head, I finally say, "I'm so sorry." When she starts to settle a little I repeat again, "I'm sorry for everything."

"Me too."

"You don't need to be sorry," I tell her shaking my head.

She pulls back and looks me in the eye. "But I am. I ruined this…us." She gazes down at our entwined bodies.

"You didn't ruin anything," I tell her. She chuckles and nuzzles back against my chest. "I mean it, Ivy, I was the one who was rude and couldn't answer your simple question."

"You don't need to," she says. "I just need you. I really want things to be just the way that they were."

"I want that too."

Neither of us says another word. As we lay together I can feel my heart steadying. That's one thing about Ivy, she calms me like no one else can. Closing my eyes, I hate myself for sleeping with Shannon last night. I should have made things right with Ivy before the wedding, but I didn't and I know better than anyone that harping on the past isn't going to change a fucking thing. So right now, I'm gonna live in this moment, with Ivy, taking each breath as though it could be my last.

Chapter 13

Waking up next to Ivy is the best feeling I've had in a long time. She sets her e-reader down and I ask, "What time is it?"

"Almost seven, you passed out and I didn't want to wake you."

"Thanks." I stretch and she takes her hand and touches the top of my head. "What happened to your hair?"

"I cut it off for the wedding, more as a 'fuck you' to my sister than anything."

"It's nice, I like it," she says.

"You think?"

"Yeah. And your face looks better."

Gently she touches it and I grab her hand, bringing it to my lips. "What happened to your place?" I ask her, concerned.

"I sort of lost it after I left your place, and haven't been able to bring myself to do much of anything."

"Did you quit your job too?"

She scrunches her eyebrows, obviously caught by my question. "No, but I missed a few days and was already on a warning for absences, so they let me go."

"Why didn't you reach out to me?"

"You were busy with the wedding and I didn't want to distract you."

"God, Ivy, I can't tell you how sorry I am."

"I knew if I missed any more days, I'd get fired, so it's my own fault. But at the time, I didn't care."

Her stomach growls, diverting my attention. "When was the last time you ate?"

She shrugs her shoulders and I look at her pissed off; the way she is acting doesn't settle well with me. She needs to take care of herself. Getting off of the bed, I head into the kitchen dodging the piles of crap along the way. Her cat meows again and I see its empty water bowl on the floor. I fill it up and it jumps down, drinking like a dehydrated camel. Opening the fridge, I look for anything that she can eat but come up empty. Her sparse cabinets aren't much better.

Walking back in her room, she's reading

again and I snatch her e-reader away. "What was that for?"

"You have NO food in your fucking house. Do you have a death wish or something?"

"Do you?" she asks me back.

I glare at her and toss her e-reader aside. Climbing on top of her on the bed, I straddle her tiny body watching the way she freezes beneath me. "You better watch your fuckin' mouth." I can't help the smile that is on my face when she nods. "I'm going to go and get some food. I want you to shower, and don't you dare get back in this bed, you understand me?"

She nods once and I kiss her forehead, leaving her panting under me.

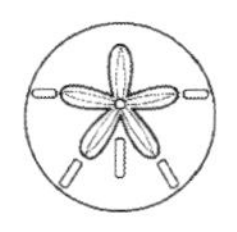

Walking back up to Ivy's apartment with my hands full of bags, I knock on the door and hear her say, "It's unlocked."

Christ!

Even after I told her to lock it behind me, she just leaves it open for anyone to stroll in.

Opening the door, I walk in and kick it closed. She is sweeping up the remnants of her destruction and I say, "I asked you to lock your door for a reason."

"And I kept it unlocked for you."

"Well, don't! Keep it locked! That's twice now that I've been able to just walk in here, which means anyone else could do the same."

She ignores my rant as I set the bags on the counter. I begin to put away the groceries, feeling bad for getting on her, but her safety is important to me. Turning on the oven, I pop the pizza in and look at her. Her wet hair is drenching through her shirt, making her nipples as clear as day. My cock twitches seeing the ridges of them peeking through. "Will you put a bra on?" I grumble. The last thing I need right now is her distracting me like that.

She looks at me and then down at my pants as she brushes all of her hair over to one shoulder. Walking up to me she takes one of my hands and cups it over her perky tit. I adjust my cock, losing my breath doing this with her. Her lips are slightly parted and my mind begins to swirl with all sorts of naughty things that I'd like to do to her. Letting go of her, I ask, "What are we doing here?" Flipping the question she asked me days ago back on her.

"I don't know. You're the one ordering me around like you own me."

"I just want what's best for you."

"Then why did you push me away last week when it wasn't good for either one of us?"

"I thought it *was* for the best. You deserve a guy that can give you the world. That guy's not me; trust me, I wish it was." She blinks a few times, hurt by my words. "I'm sorry, I'm only trying to be honest."

"I know you are and I don't mean to push things, but I feel differently. Losing Zoë brought us together and I believe for a reason. It's her pushing us towards one another. I want to see where this could go, what we could be together."

"Ivy, I want that too, more than I think you know. But I also can't risk ruining our friendship over it. You mean too much to me. When I'm not with you, I'm fucking lost. I don't like the person I become."

"Krane, nothing will ruin our friendship. That's the basis of who we are together."

Taking my hand, I run it up the middle of her chest, until I am cradling the side of her face. I contemplate kissing her slightly parted lips, but I am reminded of the risks and worry what it'll do to us. We are both breathing heavily. She smells amazing, driving me mad, and then the oven dings and it jolts me back to reality.

The moment…ruined.

Pressing my lips to her forehead, I let out a deflated breath. Pulling away from her makes my heart hurt, but something inside of me is telling me that it's the right thing to do. However, Ivy pulls me back to her, holding on to me by the sides of my t-shirt.

Her eyes are pleading me to her lips, and what she wants couldn't be clearer. "Kiss me," she whispers.

With trembling hands, I pull her body close to mine. My chest is heaving up and down like I'm about to jump off a building. "Please," she begs and I move in slowly. Letting this moment burn into my memory forever. The room is spinning as we are grounded in the middle of it. Her warm body feels amazing in my grip.

Closing my eyes, I try to move forwards, but can't close the distance. I'm not sure what is stopping me, maybe it's Zoë, even though my mind feels clear of the past right now. But I can't move. Then she kisses me and the second that our mouths touch, a passion ignites inside of me. I mold my lips around hers, the sensation so good it hurts.

Looping my fingers into the back of her hair, I hold her to me as our tongues intertwine. She tastes of mint mixed with a twist of her scent, and as much as I want to carry her to her bedroom and never stop kissing her, it's best not to push things. This is a very fine line that we are walking and both of us have to be careful with how we proceed. Because if we did not have each other, I'd be terrified for what the future will hold.

Chapter 14

"I seriously cannot believe that you made me watch that movie," Ivy complains as the credits roll along the screen.

"What do you mean?" I ask, offended that she would even say that.

"Krane, what in the world would make you think that I would like a documentary like that?"

"It's based on a bestseller," I argue.

"I don't care what it is, it sucked," she states and sits up off of my lap. I don't like the feeling of not having her close. "Come back." I pat my legs and she lies back down, picking her messy brown hair up and spanning it over my thighs. I grab the remote and turn the TV off. I need to talk to her about cleaning out the apartment in the city. It's been eating me up and I have no doubt she can shed some clarity on things.

Running my fingers through her hair, she

looks up at me and asks, "What's the matter?"

"I got a call this morning from the place in New York. The lease is up at the end of the month and they need me to move everything out."

"Can you sign another lease to give you some time?"

"I could, but the rent is going up almost seven hundred dollars a month and I can barely afford to keep it as it is now, and that's been with me accepting every fight call that I've gotten. If that lets up at all, I'll lose it."

"Fuck," she says.

"I know."

"So what's your plan?"

"I don't know. Thinking about all of our stuff there puts me into a whirlwind of anxiety. I don't think I can do it, Ivy."

"Don't say things like that, Krane. You can do anything. You have to. I'll help too."

"I don't want to put that burden on you."

"It's not a burden. Zoë would do it for me in a heartbeat. We both need to live more like her. I've been trying, that's why losing my job hasn't bothered me so much. Zoë lived believing that everything happens for a reason, and we will be better off if we live that way as well. I'm sure my mom would be happy to come and help too."

"Ivy, your mom fucking hates me."

"No, she doesn't."

I roll my eyes at her, knowing what's true. Her mom, Brenda, holds me responsible for Zoë's death. She might not come out and say it, but she does. I can't blame her though; if it were my daughter, I'd put the fault on someone else too.

"You can ask her if you want, but I don't think she'll come."

"She will. What are you planning to do with all of her stuff?"

Running my hands over my face, I get a flashback of Zoë in our apartment, painting; she loved it there. It was always her dream to move to the city, and when we did, her life was complete. "I'm not sure." I shake my head answering and move a little in my seat, but still keep her head on my lap. "I was hoping you could help me decide."

"What if we hire someone to box everything up and put it in storage?" she asks.

"I thought of that, but it'll just be a band-aid to the problem. Eventually, I'm going to have to face things."

Ivy sits up and kneels next to me. I look at the empty indentation in my lap again and she tilts my chin towards her. "We'll go through her things one at a time, together, just you and I, then my mom can come help, okay?" I'm not sure how she is as strong as she is. I nod, wanting her plan to be as easy as she makes it sound. But know having to actually do it is a whole other thing.

Ivy crawls on top of my lap and wraps me in her arms. I hold her, the closeness settling me, and I wonder how she can calm me the way she does. She makes everything so much better. All of the bad shit is gone and it's just her and I.

I yawn and it signals that I need to get home. It's been a long day, after an even longer weekend. "I'm gonna get going."

"Why?" she asks, confused.

"'Cause it's late and I am tired as hell. I need to get some sleep." She nods quickly, like I've caught her off guard. "So do you."

"I know. I just like having you here, that's all. You can stay the night, if you want."

I think about her suggestion and don't know if I can handle sleeping in the same house as her.

My cock is already on edge from touching and kissing her. It'll probably come if she looks in its direction again. "Stay," she whispers, kissing my neck and along my jaw. Being like this with her is something that I am not used to. And guilt still surges in me, insisting that I must be betraying Zoë with every touch. But Zoë is gone, and Ivy is right –she would want me to find a way to carry her love and our memories with me as I move forward into who I'm meant to be. And I love the feelings Ivy gives me.

God, give me the strength to sleep tonight and not fuck the shit out of her all night long.

"Okay, you talked me into it." And I'm instantly rewarded with her lips. The affection sends a wake up call to my dick. I battle in my mind to keep it tamed, but as she squirms on top of me, moving her pussy all over me, it's too late.

I've fought my feelings for her for long enough. We are together right now for a reason and clearly nothing can change that. But I also fear doing more than this will ruin our friendship. "Stop," I plead as she continues to kiss me.

"Why?"

"Because, I—"

"Doing this won't change things, I promise."

She reads my mind as she looks me in the eye, and as much as my body is telling me to fuck her over and over again, my brain is screaming at me not to. Her warmth on top of me is something that I need right now, but not at the risk of losing her.

Chapter 15

I can see the pain in Ivy's face as she lies next to me. It kills me that I did this to her, but something wouldn't let me move forward last night and love her the way that she deserves. Staring up at the stark white ceiling, I wonder if we had fucked, would things be just as awkward?

Scooting closer to Ivy, I pull her body against mine, but she stiffens—the affection from yesterday has vanished. Like everything else in my life, I've fucked this up too. "I'm sorry," I tell her, like an apology is really going to make a difference. It's a little too late for that now.

"Me too," she says.

Holding her in my arms feels so right; that's how I know that I did what I had to. I need her, this connection. I can't be without it.

"Is it because I'm not Zoë?" she asks me. Her question immediately catches me off guard.

What the fuck is going through her mind?

"God, no, Ivy. Why would you ask me that?"

"Why wouldn't I?"

Letting out a deep sigh, I contemplate how to answer this. "In a way, it is because you aren't her. You're the exact opposite. Yes, we've bonded over losing her, but when I am with you, it's one of the only times that my mind is completely clear of the turmoil that I have faced. I don't want to lose that. This last week apart was horrible. I drank worse than I ever have and I wasn't myself. I've made a lot of mistakes in life, especially since I lost Zoë and I'm scared that if we push things too fast and do something that neither of us can take back or one of us regrets, it'll be our demise. Then, I don't know what I'll do."

"So is that what sleeping with me will be, just a regret?"

Flipping her onto her back, I cradle her face gently in my palms. "A regret is the last thing in this world that you are. You're the only bit of light that I have left."

Scrunching my eyebrows together, I lean down and crash my lips against hers. She accepts my kisses, and yet again the closeness puts my body into overdrive. Everything that has been asleep for so long awakens, Ivy stimulates me on a different level than anyone else. The thought of being with her for the first time has my heart pounding, and I actually feel safe letting my guard down. Reaching under her t-shirt I slide my hand up her hot body and grip hard on her tit, causing her to cry out. She parts her legs and I scoot on top of her. Our tongues are a jumbled mess. Mixing and weaving together, every stroke sends a jolt of ecstasy to the tip of my dick.

Our bodies line up and I push my hard dick against her. Her wet panties make my cock drip for her. "Is this what you want?" I ask ripping the covers off the bed and looking down at us.

"Yes."

I push her shirt up, letting her flawless tits free, admiring their beauty. Then as I take my lips and wrap them around one of her nipples, she runs her fingernails up my back and I slow down, taking my time teasing her. If we are going to do this, we're doing it my way. She moans again and I tell her, "Let me hear what I do to you."

She whines louder and I pull away, bracing my weight above her. My cock is throbbing for her and I press the head of my shaft against her.

"Tell me you want me."

"I want you!"

God, she turns me on.

Even with some clothing separating us, I know being inside of her will be the best feeling in the entire world. Grinding my dick along her clit I say, "Tell me nothing will change."

"You know it won't."

"Tell me!" I growl.

"Nothing will change, Krane."

Moving my body next to hers, I kiss her neck and snake my hand inside of her panties.

Christ, she's fucking wet.

Her smooth pussy excites me. Needing to see it, I remove her underwear and stare down at her soft, white skin. Running my eyes up her body, her t-shirt is pulled above her tits and from there down she is bare. Running my thumb back and forth over her clit, she keeps her eyes on me. Trailing them all over my tattooed body.

She runs a hand down my side and tugs on my boxers. "Take these off."

I don't like letting go of her, but freeing my cock is invigorating. Sitting up she grabs my dick, stroking it, and by the way she touches me I know this will be an incredible orgasm. I watch her eyes as her lips mold around the end of my shaft and then slowly descend down it. Being in this moment with Ivy makes everything worth it.

I hold her hair out of the way so I can see her lips, so stretched and moist as she sucks me. Each movement is met with the twist of her grip, and after this, I'll never have another woman's lips on me. My balls are tight as I ask her, "Do you want my cum?"

She pulls away, still stroking me, and I place my hand over hers to cease her movements. She kneels with me on the bed and leans into my neck kissing and sucking a little along the way and says, "In my pussy."

"What?" I ask, making sure that I heard her clearly.

"I want your cum inside my pussy. I'm on birth control, so no condom. I want to feel every bit of you."

She takes her shirt off before leaning back. Reaching down with a free hand, she makes large circles over her pussy and I'm doomed. I'll last about thirty seconds inside of her.

I grip my dick hard watching her like this. She begins to moan rubbing herself faster and I pull her hand away lining my cock up with her.

My breathing is fast and I move slowly as I enter her body. Every inch feels more amazing than I've ever imagined.

Ivy grips the sheets, crying out in enjoyment, and once I am nestled all the way in, I tell her, "Don't come, whatever you do, don't come 'til I say so."

"Why?"

"Because I want to enjoy you." I back out a little and then slam into her.

"Fuck!" she screams.

"When you come, I'll lose it, okay?"

She nods her head quickly and I hold her face in my hands. Kissing her tenderly, just like the slow long movements of my dick in and out of her. She feels so fucking good that everything inside of my body almost hurts.

Her legs are slacked to the sides and I raise myself above her, watching what my cock does to her. Every thrust bounces her perky tits. Her eyes are closed and she moves her hand, getting a hard grip on one of her nipples. "Oh fuck!" I groan as she pinches it hard.

I can't watch her like this. Pulling out of her heavenly slit that is fiercely holding me inside of her, I flip her over. Her back is gorgeous as she arches in the sexiest way. She wiggles her ass for me and I grab a handful of it, as I guide myself back into her.

This angle is so much deeper. Squeezing her hard, I remind myself to let up and take my time. Slowing down to control the urge of coming, she wiggles, meeting my movements and I stay frozen. "Mhhh, that's it, fuck me," I order her. Right away she pushes upwards and is screaming on her hands and knees, "Oh my God, Krane!"

My hands can't help but roam her body and when she starts to shake a little, like she's about to come, I hold on to her, ceasing all movement. "Don't come, not yet."

She nods and lies completely still underneath me. Taking both of her hands, I pin them together above her head, and then gradually, I begin to move. With her outstretched body beneath mine and in my full control, I stroke myself just how I want.

My cum is brewing, from deep inside of me. Every nerve ending is igniting on all cylinders. "Let go," I order her and wait for her noises to pitch. They do, right as the first shot of cum fills her, unleashing an animal from inside of me.

I pump myself into her vigorously, fiercely

grunting, holding her flat against the mattress loving the way her body comes underneath mine. She rattles and shakes, holding my cock like a vice. Then when the last bit of cum leaves me, I cannot slow my movements, so I release her hands, bracing my weight by her sides and continue to smash into her.

"Oh, Krane!" she screams reaching for anything to hold on to as I come again, a violent blow filling her. Ivy lets go right along with me. Our bodies working so well together, like they were meant to be one. Both of us experience the world's greatest pleasure, brought together by the most horrific grief, and for some strange reason we've found an acceptance within the boundaries of our relationship. A blessing from Zoë rings in my mind, as her words replay like a broken record, again and again.

Everything happens for a reason.

Chapter 16

"How long do you typically run for?" Ivy asks me as we stretch at Long Beach before a run.

"Usually 'til I can't feel my legs or breathe."

"Shut up," she says and swats me.

"It's the truth," I respond blocking her.

"I'd like to feel my legs and keep breathing, if that's okay?"

"Well, today I would too," I respond and kiss her on the lips. A gesture that is so new to me, but feels so right.

"Ready?"

We head down the beach, the warm sun just greeting the day. I haven't ever been here this early, but Ivy said we had to see the sunrise. The waves crash along the shore and I look over at her running, and I couldn't be happier.

We run for only a few minutes and then she stops and I look at her puzzled. "What?"

She points to the sun as it crests the horizon. My eyes are drawn to it and I am shocked with how fast it rises. Wrapping an arm around her, I hold Ivy close to me. Breathing in her intoxicating scent. The wind whips her ponytail and I grab it in my hand, holding it in place. I can see the smile on her face as she rests her head on my shoulder.

The sun comes fully into view and I pull her hair, turning her face towards mine. "Thank you for everything," I tell her, needing to get that out in the open. She has done so much for me…for us.

She presses her lips against mine and looks at me with those eyes. The same eyes that made me fuck her yesterday. "Thank you."

"Don't look at me like that."

She smirks like she's doing nothing wrong and goes to run off. I pull her back by the hair and say, "Don't ever run from me."

"I won't."

We continue our run, neither of us saying much, but we both are enjoying being here. In this place, a place that keeps us close to Zoë, the person whom we both love and who ultimately brought us together.

"Have you thought anymore about when you want to go to the city?" she asks me as we get back to my truck.

I shake my head, resting my hand on her door handle before I open it. "Never," I respond. Knowing that going back there is only going to mentally fuck with me and possibly make me question everything that I am doing.

"Let's go today?"

Looking into her eyes, I'm unable to answer. Gently I close her door and walk around to my side. Looking out at the vast ocean on the way, it's beautiful, and for the first time since I lost Zoë, I don't say, *until tomorrow, beautiful.* I'm not sure why the words don't leave my mouth, but they just don't feel necessary.

Leaving here with Ivy is like a part of me has let go of Zoë. And though it should maybe be counterintuitive, I feel her approval. Getting into the truck, Ivy is looking at me concerned and asks, "You okay?"

"Yeah. Are you serious about going to the city today?"

"If you're ready, then I am. I know my sister and can hear what she would tell us to do. Her belongings, as much as they hold memories, they aren't her. You and I know who she was and we have to remember what she would want. She wouldn't want this to burden us any longer; she would want us to be happy."

"Okay, let's go then." Starting up my truck, we head into the city. Ivy is absolutely correct. The apartment holds a lot of memories, but so does my head, and no one can ever take that away from me.

After an hour of driving, we arrive. Pulling into the garage for the apartment, Ivy is asleep. I put the truck in park and run my knuckles down her cheek. "Wake up, Ivy."

She looks around the dark garage and then at me a little confused. "Did I sleep the entire drive?" she asks.

"Uh huh."

Her stomach growls and I stall with proceeding upstairs, using the excuse. Just being back here is fucking hard. "Come on, let's get you something to eat before we go in." We get out of the truck and the second that my feet hit the ground, I'm taken back to the day that Zoë and I moved in. She was so happy and excited. Riding up the same elevator to the lobby with Ivy, I can't help but get lost in my thoughts.

The doors ding and we exit into the bright and vibrant place that at one time I called home. The familiarity is hard to take in and I grab Ivy's hand, leading her across the lobby and out the doors. The second that we hit the New York City air, my breath comes back to me.

"Why the rush?" Ivy asks as I drag her away from the building.

"Shit, I'm sorry," I respond and slow down. "I just need to eat."

"Okay." She walks a little faster to keep up with me and then we enter the first café that I see.

Ivy and I order and then sit outside. As we wait for our food, I'm in a cloud, haunted by so many things from the past. Things that I never thought would come back to me. Like the way the marble flooring in the building reminds me of Zoë and how it made her feel our place was over the top or how the sounds of the sirens in the distance take me back to that night. My mind swirls like a fucking tornado and I'm not sure how to stop it. Looking out at all of the people as they buzz by, Ivy takes my hand and says, "If you aren't ready to do this, we don't have to."

Looking into her eyes, I appreciate the concern. She reads me well. "I...I didn't know I was going to feel her so much going back there."

Tears fill her eyes and she lets go of my hand. "Don't do that," I beg, reaching for her hand. She holds it and as we look into each other's eyes, I'm reassured that no matter what I have to face in front of me or what obstacles are ahead of me, as long as I have Ivy, I'll be okay.

"Krane, I'm sorry I said we should do this today."

"Don't be. This isn't your fault, you're just trying to help. It's me. I'm all over the place. I need to remember what is real and stay grounded."

All I can do right now is to live in the moment. I cannot get ahead of myself, because that just lets things get out of control. Each moment, each breath, each second is all I can focus on moving through.

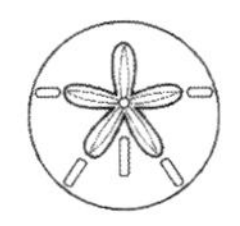

"Krane!" my name is called out as Ivy and I leave the café and I look up to see Logan walking towards us.

"What's up, man?" he asks energetically.

"Not much," I respond, "You remember Ivy." They shake hands and he looks down at our intertwined fingers, then smiles at me.

"You doing okay, brother?"

I nod and it brings him a smile. "Good. Hey, I was just headed to the gym. You should come."

"I would, man, but we gotta get—"

"No, we don't," Ivy chimes in and I give her that look. "We can spare an hour."

"For real?" Logan shouts like a girl and when I see his excitement, I feel terrible for turning my back on him. He is my best friend. We were together every day, training hard. Sometimes, I thought that he wanted me to make it even more than I did.

"Sure, man," I add.

"The guys are gonna love seeing you."

"You training with anyone?" I ask as the three of us start to walk together.

"Not really. I've mainly been helping Ethan."

"You?"

"Nah, you know I wouldn't do that."

As we round the corner, the gym comes into view and it brings a smile to my face. I have so many good memories here. This was my home away from home. This place has made some great fighters and I'm proud to say that I'm one of them.

"How long did you guys train for?" Ivy asks.

Logan stops walking and looks between the two of us. "Almost four years."

We continue on as I say, "It was a great ride. I was training for the fight of my life when we last were together, but…" I trail off. "I never made the fight."

Logan opens the door for me and the noises invade my senses. My eyes bounce everywhere, scanning all of the faces, some I recognize, while others I don't. Logan whistles, like he used to when I would slack off on training and my ears ring along with everyone else's. All eyes are pulled in my direction, and when the guys I trained with for so long recognize me, I am bombarded.

"Holy shit, Hensley's back," Ethan, the owner, yells, and the next hour is spent reminiscing. I never realized how much I missed this place, or these guys, but I do.

"A hundred bucks says not one of you pussies can stand one round in the ring with

Hensley," Ethan challenges, and then looks at Ivy and apologizes for the pussy reference.

"I'll have him tapping in half a round," a guy about my size says from across the gym.

"Don't do it, Brock," one of the guys says.

Ivy's hand is still in mine and typically I'm not egged on by anyone, but this asshole has kept quiet my entire visit, like I am sand in his underwear, and every time I've looked at him, his eyes are on Ivy.

I squeeze her hand once before letting go and then step forward. A low roar of cheers erupts in the room and the douchebag hops off the weight bench like he's tough. Pulling my shirt over my head, I toss it to Ivy and step to him.

Ethan jumps between us holding us apart. "We're not bare knuckle fighting. Suit up."

"Nah, fuck that shit!" I shout and move around Ethan pushing the guy backwards.

"You think you're tough?" he asks.

"Yeah, and you're about to find out how tough I am." I push him out of my way and hop into the makeshift ring that I have grappled and sparred in so many times. Leaning down I stretch my back and legs and then raise my fists.

"Lock the door," Ethan shouts and jumps

into the ring, holding us apart "If I let you fight like this, when I call it, you're done, understand?"

I nod once and catch sight of Ivy watching me as I pound my fists together. Having her close to me again while I fight feels good. Especially because this time I know that she is safe. Ethan steps back and says, "Bring it on."

The ten guys in the room erupt in cheers, but through it all, Logan's voice is loud and clear. I hear him better than anyone; hell, I trust him the most. As we size each other up and land a few jabs here and there, I get my feet in a good flow, but he wants to take me to the ground to try and end it quickly, and I'm not having that weak ass shit. I'd rather beat the shit out of him for four and a half minutes and then make him tap.

Swinging in for a left hook, he ducks and catches me with an uppercut. Blood pools in my mouth and I smile at him, taking things up a notch. I keep him close to the ropes as I work him around the ring, landing shot after shot. He grunts from every punch, tiring out quickly, and the satisfaction of quickly having the advantage only ramps up my adrenaline.

Stepping back, I look at him and can see the pain in his face as he heaves for air. Clearly he's not well trained in endurance. Kicking his feet out from underneath him, I contemplate my next move, then Logan sees an opportunity that I don't and shouts, "Arm bar." And I grab his arm, outstretching it in my grip. Holding it back in just the right position, I strain his elbow so I put enough pressure to make him tap, but not enough to snap it, even though I want to. I lock eyes with Ivy and watch the grin spread across her face. His groans are painful as he holds out and I tweak his arm back a little harder, then feel his free hand tapping me over and over.

Ivy claps as Ethan calls it. Jumping up and down, she raises both hands high in the air excited. Letting go of my grip, the douchebag falls off of me and I get to my feet, hugging Logan as he congratulates me along with the rest of the guys in the gym. Being back here shows me how much I've missed everyone. It was stupid of me to turn my back on these guys when I was in need of them most. But in doing so, it turned me towards Ivy and as she wraps her arms around me, I feel deep in my bones that everything I've been through has brought me to this moment. Because everything happens for a reason.

Chapter 17

"I'm proud of you for today," Ivy says. I look at her a little confused, not sure what she could be proud of me for. I completely bitched out on even going into my old apartment. "Don't look at me like that."

"I'm sorry, I don't understand why you would say that."

"Uhh, you kicked that guy's ass in the ring. You know, I really love watching you fight. I can see how happy it makes you. It's in your blood and to see you reconnect with those guys was really awesome. I'm glad that we went."

"That's nice of you to say, but we didn't get done what we needed to."

She walks over to me and wraps her arms around my waist. "And that's okay, we can do it another time. You really can't put so many expectations on yourself. Sometimes you have to just be in the moment and let what happens happen. Today wasn't meant for us to go through the apartment. We had no boxes, or a storage unit lined up, so it would have been a waste."

Looking down, I nod, agreeing with her. She is right, she always is, and I need to remember that more often. Listening to her words and staying in *this* moment, I press my lips against hers. The sensation immediately calms me. Holding her head so tenderly, I kiss her, allowing our bodies to take us where they want.

She puts so much passion into her kisses. The way her hands roam my body and her pussy brushes against my cock, mixed with the moans of her pleasure, it all turns me on. Grabbing the hem of her shirt, I lift it over her head, breaking our kiss for just a brief moment. Then I unclasp her bra freeing her perfect tits.

"I. Need. You," I whisper in between kisses.

She weaves her hand into the front of my shorts and says, "Then fuck me." Wrapping those five delicate fingers around my shaft, she strokes me, and I push my shorts down and out of the way. I fumble with her pants to get them unzipped and once I do, she steps out of them.

Then I swoop her up, carrying her to the couch, where I lay her down. Tearing my shirt above my head, I look into her eyes and remind myself to just take my time. As I lean down and inundate her body with kisses, I press my lips on every grain of her sensitive skin causing her to twitch beneath me.

Pulling back, I adore her beauty. I'll never get enough of it, or her. My dick has waited long enough. As I clench the base, I ease my way inside of her. She accepts me, like we've fucked a million times. The inside of her cunt sends a shiver down my body. Tucking my chin to my chest, I take a moment to compose myself.

She grips my ass, urging me to move, so I begin to fuck her, working every inch of myself in and out of her. With every pull and push, I groan. The feeling is un-fucking-believable. She lets out a loud whine and I look down as Ivy has her chin pointed to the ceiling and is gripping my biceps. My tattoos look dirty against the perfection that is her porcelain skin.

Her breathing is harsh, her skin blotchy, and it's the sexiest thing I've ever fucking seen. "Yes, Krane, like that."

"You like to take my cock, don't you?" I ask

her, picking up speed and grabbing both of her tits. I play with her nipples getting lost in this great world that we create together. My shaft pummels in and out of her, and I'm lost in the solace that is the connection I feel with her.

Finally, she looks at me. Her wide eyes are so hot and I cannot control myself. Letting go of her tits, I lift her hips, and slowly push into her as deep as I can. As she moans underneath me, we both freeze and I hold my dick deep inside her, rocking my hips a little, stroking that sweet spot. "Fuck!" she shouts, trembling, reaching, and gripping for anything she can.

"That's it, take my cock."

"YESSS!" Her word switches to a scream followed by her letting go and I make her come hard. Watching her like this sets me off, and I wait as long as I can, holding and savoring my orgasm. Rubbing myself inside of her wet and tight pussy is the best feeling ever.

She is still coming when it hits me, as a fiery blast of cum ignites from my balls and drenches her insides. I remind myself to keep control, to savor her and this moment. Slowing my movements I get lost in her kisses and when we finally break with my dick still inside of her she says, "I love when you make me come."

I give her one more kiss before I ease my way out of her and respond, "I love making you come. And fucking you and seeing you naked." My cock starts to grow and she looks down, giggling at me. "I can see that."

Hopping off of the bed, I walk into the bathroom and turn on the shower. I look over my shoulder and see Ivy strutting towards me. Stepping aside I gesture her in ahead of me. The warm water surrounds our bodies as I close the door behind us.

Looking into her eyes, she is so beautiful. I feel very lucky to be in this moment – she is unlike anyone else in this world. And for me to have found such a connection with her, especially after losing Zoë, is unreal.

Chapter 18

"What's that?" Ivy asks as I hold Zoë's favorite college sweatshirt out in front of me.

Turning, I show her the faded navy blue hoody and it brings a smile to her face. "Oh that's definitely a keeper. I can picture her wearing it."

"Me too," I say and pass it to Ivy, so she can pack it in one of the boxes of stuff that we are keeping in storage. This is all a lot to mentally process. But after struggling for days regarding when we would get back over here, we decided to schedule it, rented a moving truck, and are just getting it done…or trying to, at least. Even though it's hurting like hell right now, we have to – Zoë wouldn't want me struggling to pay for an empty place to keep a bunch of materialistic stuff.

"It was nice of the guys to help," Ivy says

from the bathroom. She's been talking a lot. I think to keep her mind busy and me too. It's a nice distraction, as I often find myself off in a daze of nonsense.

"Yeah, it was." Logan and a couple of buddies from the gym came by earlier today, they moved all the big stuff out of here for us and into the storage unit. Finishing up the last of the bedroom, I head into the bathroom to check on Ivy. She is sitting on the floor, surrounded by a mess of stuff.

"How's it going?"

"It's okay. You have a lot of hair products."

I smirk running my fingers over my shaved head and she smiles at me. "I'm gonna run these boxes down and check the meter."

"Okay." She looks back down going through the rest of the stuff from under the sink. Grabbing two boxes from the kitchen, I take the elevator down and let out a breath of air that I seem to have been holding.

The sun has set and today has exhausted me, probably more than I've realized. Loading the boxes into the back of the U-Haul, I'm spent. To think of unloading everything into storage and then making the trip home is unbearable, so I'm grateful I booked a hotel in the city.

I haven't had a lot of extra money lately after the underground fights have slowed, but a night to decompress after a hard day is just what we both need. Plus, it will be a good surprise for her. I pop a few more quarters into the meter and check the tires to make sure the meter man hasn't marked them. Heading back upstairs, Ivy has the bathroom all cleared out. "You want me to take these?" I ask.

"Yeah," she responds, gathering the rest of the trash leaving the floor bare.

After a few trips, the U-Haul is loaded and as I stand in the middle of what was once my home, I look around at all of the nail holes in the walls from Zoë's paintings. She was an amazing artist and had covered these walls with so many colorful pictures that had her personality shining through them.

"We did good," Ivy says intertwining her fingers with mine.

Bringing her hand to my lips, I respond, "Yeah…yeah, we did."

"Are you gonna miss it here?"

I think about all of the memories that were created in this place and am so glad that those are forever mine and locked in my head. With an honest expression on my face, I look at Ivy and respond, "No, I won't."

She tilts her head, perplexed by my comment and I let go of her hand removing the door key from my key ring. As the silver key spins around and around, I say to Ivy, "This hasn't been my home for quite a while. I'm ready to let it go."

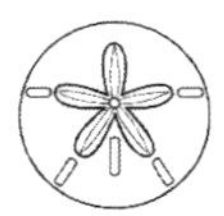

"Where are you going?" Ivy asks, as I miss the exit for the turnpike and continue towards the hotel.

"You'll see."

I can see her looking at me out of the corner of my eye. She yawns and I ask, "You tired?"

"Uh huh."

"Did you ever talk to your mom about helping with the apartment?" I ask her a little too late, but the thought that she wasn't involved just popped into my mind. She doesn't answer and I look at her. "Ivy?"

"No."

"Why not?"

"Every time I talk about you, she…she clams up."

"I don't give a shit, don't you think she would have liked to have been given the chance to be there? Besides, I told you she hates me."

She chuckles. "Well, it's a little too late now."

I glare at her, turning deeper into the city and she asks again, "Where are we going?"

"Be patient."

"Uhhhh!" She rests her tired head back in frustration. "Well, the bag of stuff that I'm keeping of Zoë's has a lot of things in it for my mom. I'm sure she'll understand."

"Will you just make sure she knows I wanted her there and that we didn't not ask her intentionally. Say we did it on a whim or something?"

"I'll handle her, Krane."

Her mom already has a bad taste in her mouth where I'm concerned and now that we did this without consulting her, although it was *my* apartment, it will elevate things if she doesn't take it well. Pulling up to the hotel, I put my truck in park and am greeted right away by a valet guy.

Ivy looks at me surprised.

"Come on, let's go decompress."

"And shower," she adds, looking down at her jeans insinuating they are dirty. I sling an arm over her shoulder and kiss the top of her hair on the way inside. "You do stink a little."

She tries to pull away from me, but I hold her close.

"Thank you for doing this for us."

"Anything for you," I tell her.

Check in is a breeze and come to find out I went to school with the guy that works the counter. As we enter the hotel room, I can see that he hooked it up for us tonight. This place is massive, everything is open and lit up. There is an expansive wall of windows that overlooks Central Park. Flipping on the fireplace as I enter the bedroom, Ivy says, "Did you book this room? I thought you told the guy at the counter you wanted a king room?"

I flop back on the bed, looking at the ceiling and respond, "This is a king's room." She lies on top of me nuzzling close, and even though today was unbearable at times, we did it. "Thank you for everything," I tell her, kissing the top of her shoulder.

"I can't believe we got it all done."

Going though the apartment and leaving it empty was a lot of work, especially to do it all in one day. But it also let me release a part of my past. Looking down at Ivy resting so peacefully across my body, it's all worth it. Her breathing is even and I hate to get up, but we need to shower.

"Stay here," I tell her and slip away. Walking into the bathroom, which is mainly made up of granite, I turn the water on to the huge soaking tub, knowing she'll love to relax for a bit. Going back out, I lift her off of the bed. "Come on, baby, up you go."

The endearment slips out of my mouth and we both look at each other. I've never said it before, and she grins as I cradle her tired body against my chest. Walking her into the bathroom, I set her next to the tub. The room is starting to fill with steam and I adjust the water before I remove her clothes, taking extra time to pay attention to all her sensitive places.

"Aren't we going to rinse off first?" she asks.

"Probably smart," I respond and turn the shower water on before I undress. Quickly we wash off and then as I hold her hand, we carefully walk on the slippery floor and she asks, "Will you just hold me?"

We both step foot into the tub and I slide down first, sitting in the hot water, which stings my skin. She stands in front of me and leans down cupping a handful of water that she picks up and runs down her body. As she bends forward, her ass and pussy are spread directly in front of my face.

"Do that again and you'll be riding my cock in here."

She looks back at me, bracing her weight on the sides of the high walls of the tub and sits in front of me. My cock is stiff and wants her, but I respect her wishes and fold my arms around her, pulling her close to me.

"Do you think you'll ever tell your mom about us?" I ask, thinking about our conversation from earlier.

"Sure, when the time's right."

"You should give your mom the picture Zoë painted of Long Beach."

She turns in my hold and blinks a few times before turning back around.

"Why?"

"Because it would make her happy."

I cannot change the animosity that Brenda has for me, or make her understand what Zoë meant to me, especially once she finds out about Ivy and I, but what I can do is follow my gut and do what I think would make Zoë happy. I remember hearing her on the phone with her mom after she painted it, she was so excited and proud. She couldn't wait to share it with her. It might be a small gesture, but right now, I'll take it. Anything I can do to show the woman who hates me most that I am not a monster after all.

Chapter 19

Looking out at the view of Central Park while I sip my coffee, the noises of honking and sirens in the distance are familiar. This moment takes me back to when I first moved here. I loved New York City, still do honestly. But being here is hard; my mind can't rest because the noises in my head are loud.

My phone rings pulling me back to the present. It's Logan. "What's up, brother?" I answer, leaning back in my chair.

"Not much, buddy, just getting into the gym and I've got a bit of a dilemma."

I take a sip of my coffee and respond, "And you're calling me? I'm probably the last person that can help anyone."

"Oh, but I think you can. Plus, you owe me one for yesterday."

"You're right. What's up?"

"Cam cracked three ribs sparring last night."

"Who the fuck was he sparring with?"

"Brock."

"You need to get rid of that guy; he's bad fuckin' news." My voice rises and I don't want to wake Ivy. Looking inside, I see her ass peeking out from underneath the sheets. She's sleeping so comfortably.

Christ, she's gorgeous.

"I know, but that's Ethan's problem."

"So what do Cam's ribs have to do with me?"

"He was scheduled to fight tonight against Ronnie Shone, for ACM. Now we have to find a replacement fighter, and Ethan and I want that to be you."

"No way, I'm down on my training and am not ready to get back out there, especially with ACM." The American Cage Maniacs is one of the top fighting companies in the US. If I were to fight for them unprepared and lose, I'd ruin any chance at a real career. "I'm sorry, but for now I'm going to have to pass."

"Come on, dude. It pays five grand, and if you win fight of the night it's an extra 2K." Fuck, I could use that kind of money. The thousand dollars here and there are nice, but it's just not enough sometimes and Ling hasn't called me for a while. Makes me worried that he got busted or something. "Please, man, Ethan and I will have your back. We wouldn't ask if we didn't think you could beat this guy. We saw you in the ring with Brock. You haven't lost one bit of your skills. I know it's short notice, but I'll have everything there for you, all you need to do is show up and fight. It's in your weight class so no cutting or anything like that. Will you at least think about it?" he asks, practically begging me.

"When do you need an answer?"

"Soon. Can you decide in the next thirty minutes?"

"Yeah, let me talk it over with Ivy, then I'll let you know."

"Great, thank you, man."

I hang up and glance inside. Ivy's lazy ass is still asleep, so I take this time to Google Ronnie Shone and see what kind of fighter he is and what his record is. He's undefeated in his last ten fights and has lost only one fight for his overall 'Big 20' Record. Pound for pound, we match up well. Going back to Google, I click on another link and read an article regarding this fight that was supposed to be against him and Cam. He's a shit talker. A mental player, like I am. Fighting him could get me back into the spotlight, and if I win, it could jumpstart my professional career, but on the other hand if I lose, it could end it all right away.

Looking in at Ivy, I contemplate what to do. I can't decide without talking to her, so I get up and go in, setting my empty cup of coffee on the table before gently lying down next to her. As I brush her hair off of her back and strum my fingers over her skin, she whimpers and says, "Just five more minutes."

"It's almost eleven, baby."

She opens her sleepy eyes and looks at me with the cutest expression. "I like when you call me that."

"I know."

I keep moving my fingers over her back again and again and she closes her eyes. "Come on. Wake up, sleepyhead," I tell her and stop moving my hand.

She moans in protest, looking at me. "Why?"

"Because we have to check out soon and I need to talk to you about something."

Her eyes open and she rolls over running her

hands over her face. Her tit pops out and I grab it, massaging it. "What's up?"

"Logan called."

"Yeah, what did he have to say?"

"He wants me to step in and fight tonight for Cam from their gym against a guy in the ACM."

"Why you?"

I fill her in on all of the details. "Am I crazy to even consider this?"

"No, this could be huge for your career."

"But I'm not even sure that I want a career, some days."

"But there are days that you are sure."

Ivy and I continue this back and forth weighing the pros and cons and after watching some of his YouTube clips I still can't make up my mind.

"It's such a risk."

"I think you should take the chance and do it," she decides.

"Why?"

"Because I know you can beat this guy. Something's just telling me you should do it."

Looking into her eyes, I can see the certainty I need. "You sure?" I ask.

She nods her head and her certainty is contagious – I can feel it too. "Okay, let me text

Logan." Taking my phone from my pocket I send a message giving him a green light. Then a rush of adrenaline that I haven't felt for a long time hits me, knowing that I'm about to step back into the world of legit fighting that I left behind.

Ivy hops off the bed and struts into the bathroom, naked and sexy. I sprawl out on the comforter waiting for her to get back, thinking about her pussy, but knowing that I can't have it, now that I am slotted to fight tonight. "The laundry's back if you wanna get dressed."

"No, thanks," she says and runs out of the bathroom, jumping on top of me. I laugh out loud as her naked body covers mine. She drenches me with kisses, grinding that delectable cunt so hard against my cock, but I have to put a stop to this. Flipping her over, I pin her beneath me and sit up. She looks puzzled and reaches inside my underwear. Taking both her hands, I hold them above her head and rub my nose against hers. "No."

"What? Why?"

"Because you made me agree to a fight tonight."

"I don't give a shit," she shouts and wiggles

underneath me.

Tightening my grip on her wrists to show her that I am serious, I repeat myself again, "Not happening."

"Why not?"

"Do you know how much energy fucking you and coming exerts? I need to save it for tonight, especially with my training being how it's been."

"So no sex?" she asks with the saddest look on her face.

"No, not until after I win, baby."

I release my grip, hating that I can't give her what she wants. I wish I could, but the ramifications if we fuck could be dire, and now she knows it too. She wants me to win just as much as I do. But I can still please her. Lifting her ass up, I scoot her up the bed and spread her legs. Her pink cunt glistens, wet for me, and I run my tongue over it, wishing that I could just slide my cock inside. To feel the walls of her surrounding me, how they tighten and expand from what I do to her. But I can't, so I settle my mouth around her clit, flicking and sucking on one of my favorite parts of her body.

She writhes and moans from my actions and

I get lost pleasing her, pushing her to the edge. I realize in this instance, how from today going forward that this is truly a fresh start for us. With making the money I could tonight, I can cover the rent at both of our places for a while. I don't want her to stress about finding another job. I just want us to be together, every day.

"Oh my God, Krane!" she screams and grabs both of her tits, pinching her nipples. I close my eyes, pushing her into an intense orgasm that has her body red from working her.

I look up at her as her eyes finally open and keep sucking her clit. She moans from the pleasure and presses herself hard against me. "Are you sure you can't fuck me?"

As I pull away, I blow a cool breath of air on her and she giggles. "Trust me, I want to…but I'm sure. Get dressed, I want to take you somewhere." She smiles and rolls over, running into the bathroom, excited in a way that I haven't seen from her in a long time. Too long.

Chapter 20

"I've always loved Central Park," Ivy says as we walk around and sip on our coffees after leaving the hotel and exploring this place. We've walked through so much of the park this morning, which has been a nice way to start the day.

"Would you ever want to live in the city?" I ask her.

She thinks about my question before responding. "Maybe if I got a job here. But I like the ocean too much. You remember that place in Long Beach I showed you the other day?"

"I remember," I tell her, recalling how she gushed about these condos last week when we went for a run.

"If I could pick anywhere, that'd be it. What about you?"

"I don't think I'd ever want to live here again. But, speaking of a job…this fight pays a good amount of money and since I no longer have the extra payment for the apartment here, I don't want you to stress about work or money or anything like that for a while, okay?"

She scrunches her eyebrows at me. "I can't let you pay for my things. I've got savings to last a while."

"You can and you will. Ivy, you're my girlfriend now and I will take care of you."

"Girlfriend?" she asks like it's a shock placing her hand over her chest. "Were you gonna run that by me first?"

"No, I wasn't 'cause you already know where we stand and when we talk about things, it just complicates the whole situation."

"Girlfriend…" she says in a quiet tone.

"Yes, accept it! Now help me clear my head for tonight. I'm starting to get anxious."

"Don't get anxious."

"Ha, that's helpful," I blurt out. "Have you looked at social media in…I don't know…the last ten minutes?"

"No, I haven't and you shouldn't either. Give me your phone." She outstretches her hand to me and reluctantly I hand it to her. However, knowing myself, it's the best decision. I need to keep focused. She slides it into her back pocket and I say, "If Logan calls, you better give it to me."

"I will, you freak."

I bust out laughing. Ivy grins, wrapping her arm around my waist and we leave the park, heading to see Logan at the gym and make a game plan for tonight. On the drive, Ivy's phone rings. "Shit, it's my mom."

"Then answer it."

She rolls her eyes at me. "Hey, Mom," she says in a chipper tone.

I can hear Brenda yelling right away and it makes me fume. How could any mother treat their daughter the way that she does, especially when she just lost one?

"I don't know," she argues back.

Brenda is yelling again and I swear I hear my name. "I'll ask him. Don't take this shit out on me."

A couple of beats of silence on Ivy's end. "No," Ivy shrieks.

Brenda yells again and I hear her say my name loud and clear. Pulling over. I snatch the phone from Ivy. She looks at me with huge eyes and I pause giving her a minute to stop me, but she doesn't. "Brenda, it's Krane," I cut her off and shut her right up. "Can you tell me why your daughter is crying?"

"Oh, you have some fucking nerve, young man. After what you did to Zoë, now you're with—"

"I didn't do anything to Zoë but try and save her, don't you fucking forget that."

"That's the last thing you did, if she hadn't been with you, she'd be alive."

"What happened to Zoë was out of our control. She died of SUDEP in my fucking arms and now I have to live with those images every day. Brenda, I get that you're in pain, but please don't take it out on Ivy."

"You can call it whatever you want, young man, or convince yourself of anything to make yourself feel better. But she was intoxicated in the middle of the night on a desolate New York City subway, alone, with you and no one else. So it's hard to not put the blame in your lap."

"Why don't you stop trying to pit the blame because nothing's ever going to bring Zoë back." My hands are shaking being forced to go back to that night. It was horrible the way her body rocked uncontrollably, the blood, the noises…everything. Then counting her final three breaths and I'm back there. Ivy wraps one of her hands around mine, pulling me back to reality and it calms me. "Do you ever try and understand who your daughter was?"

"I know who she was goddammit," Brenda screams through a sob. "Stay away from Ivy, Krane, I mean it."

"I'm sorry…but I can't."

Chapter 21

"One eighty-one and a half," Logan says and I hop off the scale.

"So you never have to cut weight?" Ivy asks me.

"Nope, not usually." I adjust the waist of my shorts and take a drink of water.

"Oh, he has before and you better watch out 'cause it's scary," Logan warns.

"What's that mean?" I ask offended.

"Uhh, that you act crazy, all agitated and moody, like a bitch."

I laugh remembering a time when I did cut weight. "That was when you made me take a welterweight fight when I'm a middleweight."

"No," he shakes his head laughing, "I didn't make you do anything. You wanted to fight that douche, remember?"

"Same difference, you encouraged me and

then let me agree to it, before I knew the ramifications."

"Whatever, you kicked his ass."

Logan puts on the sparring gloves and I hop up, punching every time he raises a hand to me. My heart is pumping strong. Even though this is the shortest notice I've ever taken a serious fight on, I cannot wait to get into the ring. As I stand toe to toe with Logan, repeatedly hitting again and again, Ivy's eyes are on me. I can't help but look at her, and Logan hits me over the back of the head. "What the fuck, man?" I yell, dropping my arms.

"You got distracted, by whatever this is." He points between the two of us. "It can't interfere with your mind tonight."

"It won't, punk." I nod, grabbing a towel and wipe the sweat off of my face. There is a light knock on the door and Logan answers it. His wife, Victoria, and Ethan enter. The girls met at Logan's birthday and seemed to thankfully connect. I mean, she hugs Ivy before me. "What am I chopped liver?" I tease her.

She smiles and hugs me. "No way, how are you feeling?"

"Really good."

Ethan and I fist bump. "You ready?" he asks.

"Hell yeah."

"Good, it's fucking nuts out there," Ethan says.

I've never been one to get nervous, the hype and adrenaline of a crazy crowd just set up an intense fight, which pumps me up. But this is Ronnie's hometown so that makes me a bit uneasy. There's another knock on the door and Ethan opens it, "Hensley, you're up in five." I take my last drink of water and put on a thin white walkout hoody. Logan was right when he said that he came with everything. He had a complete fight kit with sponsors and everything on the clothes.

Ivy stands, putting her hands in her back pockets. The look in her eyes is a little off.

"You okay?" I ask, seeing that she's clearly nervous. Stepping to her, I place my hands on her hips waiting for a reaction. "Don't stress, baby."

The room quiets from my words, but I don't care. She looks down at the ground and shakes her head. "Hey." I lift her chin bringing her eyes to meet mine. "I mean it, Ivy, I need you cheering me on. You hear me?"

She nods and I pull her against my body. Leaning down I kiss her hard, after being deprived of her lips for far too long. The room silences, our affection catching everyone off guard. I can imagine all of their eyes on us. As she pulls away, her expression has changed, the nerves from earlier have vanished. There is a knock on the door and Ethan opens it. "You guys are up," a short stocky guy says.

"Tell me you got this," Ivy requests.

"You know I do, baby." I take her hand in mine and we all head out into the hallway. The noise of the crowd as we round the short corner ignites a fire inside me. I might be first out, but this is my fucking night. The crowd is roaring and as I emerge, the room erupts in the low rumbles of booing. I've always been a fan favorite, so this reaction is not what I'm used to. But this is Ronnie's hometown and the crowd is making that known. Ivy squeezes my hand and then the girls veer off to their seats while Logan, Ethan, and I continue on. "Remember to keep your hands up and use your kicks," Logan says as the ref checks my hands and arms before giving me the green light to enter the cage.

I hug them both before bolting up the stairs

and take my side in the octagon. The song changes in preparation for Ronnie's arrival. With my back to the entrance, I listen to Logan and Ethan as they stand over the cage. The crowd chants Ronnie's name – waiting.

"You got this, Krane!" Ethan shouts.

I nod, hearing his words and turn around looking for Ivy. This will be the last time that I can look at her until this is over. She and Victoria are seated surrounded by the guys from the gym. I feel safe knowing that they will keep an eye out for her. We connect eyes and I give her a wink as the MC announces Ronnie's entrance. Everyone goes wild and then my eyes are glued on his as his are to mine. He runs to the cage, restless to get inside, moving and weaving as the ref checks him, then in two swift steps he's up the stairs. But I hold my ground, not giving in to his aggression. I know the rules for a fight of this caliber. I cannot lunge at him or get crazy like I can get away with in the underground world. Instead, I watch him, studying everything about him, focusing on the way that his hands move as he air boxes and how he plants his feet.

He's a striker, so I know that I have to take this to the ground. The ref calls us to the center and states the rules, then asks, "Are you ready?" I nod once and he asks Ronnie the same. When he agrees, round one begins. I hone in on Logan's voice, like I always have, his words my key to a victory. But before I can react to anything he's telling me, a kick flies over my head. I duck, barely missing it, and attack back. We battle standing up, each of us sizing the other up, landing a few bombs here and there.

I get in a good right hook, but he retaliates landing a left. Both of us stay composed, neither struggling for air, and I settle in for a long one.

"Use your legs," Logan reminds me and I start to mix in leg shots in between my jabs. He's a shit talker too, but I don't listen to his words. Logan's voice is the only one that I hear. I land a solid body shot, but he gets me hard in the cheek. We continue working each other over and over again, and before I know it the ten-second bell dings and then I'm in the corner with Logan and Ethan. Logan rests a bag of ice on my shoulders while Ethan cleans my face up. "You have to get him to the ground. You don't want this to go the full three rounds standing up." I nod, taking a drink of water that I spit out.

Even if I give it my all standing up, he's just

as good as I am, if not a little better. "Use your leg, that's your weapon, man."

The break is over and as much as my head is in this fight, I still can't wait for it to be over so I can be alone with Ivy. I can't help the smile that's spread across my face thinking of her. Round two begins and I focus more on my kicks to try and take him to the mat. He's relentless though and in a last ditch effort, I press him against the cage, tiring him out with as many body shots as I can throw, doing my best to take him off his feet. The round ends and I'm pissed with myself.

Fuck!

"Don't get frustrated, man. This is your round – now go end this shit."

Beginning round three, I can see the exhaustion starting to sink in for Ronnie; his hands are lower than they have been the entire fight. Maybe he's not that well trained in endurance. Either that, or he's being cocky.

Hitting him backwards, I guide him to the cage. Then holding my forearm tightly to his neck, I reach down and grab between his legs instead of taking his feet from underneath him.

This is do or die. With all of my strength, I grip hard, lifting him as high as I can. The room goes silent as I prepare to drop him, Logan and Ethan are yelling encouragement. As I throw him down, following his body to make sure that I get on top, he lands in the most awkward way on his neck, clearly stunned but not knocked out. Taking side control, I lay elbow after elbow, watching him curl up and become defenseless. The crowd roars, urging him to get up, and it's not but another ten seconds of this before the ref calls it. I hop off of Ronnie, screaming like a fucking animal with every muscle in my body flexing. Jumping on the side of the cage, I hug Logan and Ethan. Looking out at the crowd, they are all pissed. Egging them on would be a real asshole move, and stupid as fuck, so I get off the fence. As I look for Ivy, she has the biggest grin on her face and it makes me so happy I fulfilled my promise to her.

I keep my interview short and then jog down the stairs to the chorus of booing. But I'm not affected by it one bit. The guys are behind me and Ivy is in my sight, but right before I make it to her, some chick throws herself at me, pulling me to her like she knows me and grabs my face planting her lips on mine. I push her away, anger burning inside of me. "What the fuck?"

"You kicked ass!" Shannon from my sister's wedding screams, drunk and stumbling.

I keep my arm held out, holding her back, but don't need to as Ivy pulls her by the back of her hair and slaps her in the face, cursing at her. I stand stunned, not sure how to intervene. Ethan lunges forward to break them up, and I put an arm up stopping him. I can't lie, I like this side of Ivy.

"I don't know who the fuck you are, you drunk skank, but Krane is mine."

Shannon cackles and sways, resting her drunk ass against the wall. The crowd is brewing behind us. "You sure about that? He was happy to fuck me at his sister's wedding."

"I'm sure he wasn't!" Ivy grabs Shannon's face as her drunk head hangs laughing. "Why don't you shut the fuck up, while I make myself clear? Stay the fuck away."

"Or what?"

Ivy punches Shannon hard in the stomach, dropping her to her knees.

"Enough," Ethan yells, "You guys go. I got this."

Taking my arm, I sling it over Ivy's shoulder and walk off. "Please tell me you didn't sleep with her."

I usher her into the dressing room and nod my head, not able to confirm the words out loud. "I'm sorry, I was drunk and you and I weren't talking and I thought that was it, we were over, and I just wanted to forget about everything for a while. I was in a fucked up place without you."

Ivy puts her hand up. "Just stop. I really don't care about what you did before we became this. But let it be known that I don't have a problem standing up for what's mine."

"I can see that, and you looked so hot doing it." Leaning down, I claim her mouth. Christ, she tastes so amazing.

"I wanna fuck you bad."

"Mmmm, me too."

Reaching behind her, I cup her ass just as Ethan barges in, and I look over Ivy's shoulder at him. "Fuck, I'm sorry, but you gotta get out of here."

"Why?" I ask confused.

"The paramedics just took Ronnie out of here on a stretcher."

"What?"

"Yeah, he was complaining of numbness in his legs or some shit like that. Just leave your stuff here, I'll get it all for you. The crowd is fucking pissed."

Logan pops his head in. "Sorry, I had to get Victoria out of here. You guys ready? Shit's getting stupid really fast out there."

"Yeah."

"Give me your keys and I'll pull your truck around." Ivy takes them out of her purse and gives them to Logan, in a hurry he jogs off. I remove the thin gloves that cover my hands and take Ivy's, holding it tightly with the tape still covering my knuckles. She lets out a loud breath of air stressing about the belligerent crowd. "Don't worry, we'll be fine. We just need to move fast."

I grab a towel, pressing it against my face as we exit the room. The hallway is clear and I notice when we round the corner heading towards the back door there is a large group of people shouting profanities. Security is just barely holding them back, and I pick up our pace.

"Let's just say that kicking ass in North Rutherford doesn't sit well with the fans," Ethan says opening the back door. I don't look back, but it sounds like the mob is getting closer, and these fuckers sound like they're out for blood.

Logan screeches up and puts my truck in park. I usher Ivy inside and then quickly hop into the driver's seat myself.

"We'll talk later," Logan says. "Ethan or I will get your money. Just get out of here."

"Thanks for everything, guys. Be safe!"

I roll my window up and speed off, seeing the first angry fans pouring out of the building, and a beer bottle comes flying at us, fortunately with shitty aim. "You okay?" I ask Ivy, sensing that she is a little shaken.

"Yeah, that was all just a lot to handle."

"It's not normally like that, but fighting in someone else's hometown can always set the tone for madness. But it's over now."

"I don't mean that."

Shit, I was hoping she'd drop the Shannon thing.

I guess my persuasion to distract her sexually only worked for a brief moment. "You have to know that sleeping with that girl meant *nothing.* It was a one-time thing. I was drunk and angry that we weren't talking. Trust me, I regret it. I should have made things right with you and taken you to Mia's wedding."

"You can't change the past. Who knows, had you done that, then maybe we would have slept together back then and then both would have regretted it happening so soon."

"I'll never regret being with you. I know that for a fact."

Ivy rests her head back and wraps her hand around mine. "Do you want me to take your tape off?"

"When we get home; for now, just hold my hand."

Chapter 22

Sitting back, I let Ivy clean my face up. She is so gentle and I love the way her eyes squint as she meticulously takes care of me. Zoë and I always had a dream that I'd make it big one day, but she'd never help me clean up after a fight; blood and shit like that creeped her out. But Ivy, she's very attentive.

We are sitting on the couch and as she kneels next to me, her tits are popping out of the thin white t-shirt. My cock is thinking very bad things, but I don't make a move, seeing how much she is enjoying taking care of me. My eyes do however scan her body, moving up and down, all over her contours. Her legs, panties, tits, everything, imagining my hands all over her.

Her phone vibrates on the table for the fourth time tonight and I ask, "Are you gonna check that?"

"It's just my mom."

"I'm sorry that I went off on her earlier."

"Don't be, she needed to hear what you said."

"I don't know about that, but I couldn't let her upset you like that."

She puts a coating of Neosporin on my cuts and then straddles my lap, resting her arms on my shoulders. "She did; she's angry and has to let go of the pain that is festering inside of her. It's not a healthy way to live. I did a while ago and that's what has got me through all of this."

"You're strong."

"I am because I have to be; that's what Zoë would want for me. I can't break down and give up, that'd be the last thing that she'd want. There have been plenty of times that I've wanted to, but I'm a survivor. I mean, we all are really, there are just different ways of showing it."

Lifting my hands I cradle her face. She blows me away every day, her strength is truly something special. "Spoken very well. Ivy…" I trail off, holding on to her as she looks back at me. She's patiently waiting for my response. I want to tell her so many things, but none of them will come out right now, so I press our lips together and move my hands down her body until I am gripping her thighs. Lifting her up, I carry her out of the living room. She laughs against my mouth as we move, and once we are in my room, I toss her on the bed.

"Get naked," I order her.

"You first," she challenges back. I drop my sweats, letting them stay bunched at my ankles and grab my dick. "Why? You want this?"

She nods, putting her hands under the sides of her panties and slowly slides them off. I watch her every move, stroking my dick as I do. "Touch yourself."

"Like this?" she asks placing her hand over her sex and slowly rubs two fingers back and forth.

Watching her play with herself turns me on like nothing else. With my hand wrapped tightly around my shaft, I stroke myself and scoot on the bed kneeling next to her mouth.

She looks at my cock and smiles. Then drops her head back and moans loudly. Reaching down with my free hand, I lift her head and guide her mouth to the tip of my dick. She's as eager as ever, pleasing herself and molding her tight lips around me. I hold on to the back of her head sliding myself in and out of her.

In the distance, my phone rings, but nothing could stop me right now. Letting go of my cock, I reach down and move her hand aside, sliding my two fingers inside her pussy. "Mmm, you're wet like a good girl."

I begin to finger her and my phone rings again. She pulls away and asks, "Do you wanna get that?"

"Fuck no!" I take her head and guide those perfect lips back around me. Her mouth is a fucking goldmine, pleasing me in the most indescribable way.

With every pull and push of my fingers, she matches it with her lips and it about makes me come. But I control myself and then pull out as she comes herself. I shake my head smiling as her body rattles under my control.

My hand moves viciously enjoying her coming and then her body slows. I roll her body to her side, backing her ass up to me. Looking down, I can see a bit of her delectable cunt and move, nudging my cock against her, then she asks, "Can I fuck you?"

She doesn't have to ask me that twice.

Lying back, I put my hands behind my head

and let her take control. She straddles me removing her shirt and exposes her perky tits. I gesture that she leans down and gives them to me, but she doesn't. She clenches my cock, burying me deep inside of her.

"Fuck," I mumble, enjoying her warmth and tightness.

She reaches up, placing her hands behind her head, holding her hair in a mound on top of her head. She makes the sexiest noises sliding up and down my cock. Everything she is doing brings me so close to coming, but I don't want to let go, so I take both of my hands and brace them on her hips, stopping her from moving. She looks at me confused. "Tits in my mouth, NOW!"

"But I like riding your cock."

"And I love your pussy." I pull her down to me, my eyes on her hard nipples. "But I don't want to come yet." I wrap my lips around her soft skin, sucking and flicking, causing her to whine in pleasure and she begins to bounce her ass, grinding her pussy on me.

The friction is so hard. Our hot and sweaty bodies are a perfect melody together and as I move to her other nipple, she slips away, sitting all the way up and fucking me hard. I watch her body and how the impact of my cock bounces her boobs.

"Fuck me, baby," I order her, feeling my orgasm starting. She moves faster and I watch her for as long as I can. The flawlessness that is her body on top of mine pushes me over and I let go, shutting my eyes tight and pumping my hips upward. She bounces downward, working against me, and I come hard, so intense and so fucking delicious that I have to flip her over, pummeling myself inside of her.

"You like it rough, don't you?" I ask, fucking her vigorously.

"Yes," she says through a labored breath, wrapping one leg around me. Leaning up, I brace my weight on one side of her, and grip her thigh with my other hand getting lost in this moment, in this desire, with Ivy. Holding on to her tightly as we fuck, nothing else matters as I am inside of her, all of the pain of our past vanishes.

Chapter 23

"Krane," Ivy mumbles into the pillow and nudges me awake.

"What?"

"Your phone."

In the distance, I can hear the ringing, but the warmth and solace of this bed are too great to get me out of it right now. "Fuck it."

The ringing stops and I pull Ivy's naked body close to mine, cuddling her. She whimpers a little and I nuzzle her neck breathing her in. She smells fucking amazing. The completeness of the moment drifts me back to sleep…

Suddenly, she shakes me awake. The god-damn ringing has started again and I rip the covers off. It's been going off since last night. "What?" I answer yelling into the phone.

"I'm sorry to call so early Krane," Logan says.

"You better fucking be, bitch." I glance at the clock, it's 6:46 in the morning.

"I am, I tried you a few times last night and didn't hear back. After you guys left last night, shit hit the fan."

"What the fuck happened?"

"Shut up," Ivy yells from the bedroom and I close the door so her lazy ass can sleep some more.

"A lot, man – the prognosis for Ronnie isn't good at all and the fans went nuts. And that wasn't even the big thing. So Ethan and I decided to get the fuck out of there, and on the way out one of the scouts for ACM approached us. They are interested in discussing your options for fighting under them. But it's gonna come with a price."

"What the fuck? I don't even know how to take all that. So first, what's up with Ronnie?"

"He can't move from the waist down."

"Shit, you're not fucking serious?" I ask, feeling terrible. I've seen shit like this go down before. It's a risk we all take, but it's always horrible.

"Yeah, it's pretty bad. I'm not sure if it's temporary or what, but it's not something anyone ever wants."

Fuck, knowing that I did this to him has my head spinning. "So what, does ACM just want me as Ronnie's replacement?"

"I don't think so, they seemed sincere in their interest. There's so much that goes into all this and beating Ronnie, with your prior record, put you in the top twenty of your weight class," he pauses and I can't imagine ranking that high.

"Regardless of where I rank, I don't want beating Ronnie until he can't fucking walk to be the launch of my career. That's fucked up."

"Come on, man, you won fair and square. He knew just as much as you did the ramifications for fighting. You always know before stepping foot in the octagon that something could go wrong."

"So what? I win the one fight that can set me up for the future, but it comes with a shit ton of guilt? I ride his tragedy to the top?"

"Don't think of it like that. Let's keep hope he'll get better. And who knows, you could have a re-match with Ronnie one day. I think that ACM is really serious about you, so what do you think about me representing you?"

"You think this is all legit?" I ask.

"Absolutely."

"You're one of the only guys in this world that I trust, so of course."

"Good, thank you, man. I'll be in touch in a bit and please don't beat yourself up. Oh yeah, I forgot to mention, I have your check for last night. You won fight of the night so you should have an extra two grand on it."

"All right, man, thanks."

Hanging up with Logan, my mind begins to process everything. I'm not sure that a career in fighting is something that I want. Especially, if I have the capability to injure someone permanently and it keeps adding to my karmic shitstorm, then fighting might not be for me after all. But there is so much possibility, if I can make a career out of it.

Fuck, I'm starting to sweat, my throat feels tight, and I cough to clear it. Me and Ronnie's hometowns aren't that far apart, and if he doesn't get better, then some dumb shit could do something and possibly hurt the ones I love and I won't risk that…I can't.

I start a pot of coffee and Google Ronnie's name to see if I can get any information on his condition. I just need a sliver of hope right now to help get my head right, but there's nothing. I don't want to wake Ivy, and as she crosses my mind, I can feel Zoë jumping into the forefront of my thoughts.

It's a hard pill to swallow imagining doing any of this without her. This was just as much her dream as mine.

Writing a note to Ivy, I leave it on the counter.

Went to Long Beach to clear my head. –K

I know what I have to do. I'm gonna need Zoë's strength to get me through this. She will be able to tell me what to do.

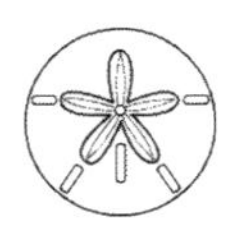

Getting home, Ivy is still sleeping and I decide to shower in hopes that will clear my mind. As the water heats the room, I look at my reflection in the mirror. My face is swollen and bruised, covered with cuts.

Going to Long Beach today didn't help me the way that I'd thought it would. I can still feel

Zoë there, but the decision ahead of me is something that Ivy and I need to make. Ivy is my future and the one who can help me decide. After this morning, it's obvious that she is the only one that can really clear my head.

Rinsing off, I look at the tub as the pink water swirls down the drain and I'm thankful that Ivy is not in here. Before getting out, I hold my breath and let the hot water cleanse my face, erasing the remnants of last night's fight. As I stand here, frozen in time, I pray that Ronnie will be okay. I don't want to ever cause anyone permanent harm, no matter what.

I wipe my body dry and then wrap a towel around my waist. Opening the door to my room, Ivy is still passed out. "Baby," I call out getting dressed.

"Nooo," she whines and pulls the covers over her head.

"Come on, you have to get up."

She ignores me. Going into the kitchen, I pour us each a cup of coffee and tell her as I go back into the bedroom, "I have something for you."

Slowly she pulls the covers off of her head and peers out at me to see what I have. I gesture the cup towards her and she huffs sitting up. "You already showered?"

Her voice is raspy and I laugh at her. "I did and went to the beach, I offered you to join, but you just cursed at me."

"No, I didn't."

I smirk, she knows me so well. Handing her the coffee, I sit down. "You're so lazy, you know that?"

She takes a sip and shakes her head at me, "No, I'm not. I'm tired. You woke my ass up in the middle of the night to fuck, so I didn't get a full night's sleep."

"Me?" I question her recalling the events that took place. "I remember waking up to your lips wrapped around my dick."

"Yeah, because you were moaning in your sleep."

"Was I now?" I ask, raising my eyebrows.

She throws a pillow at me and asks, "Who was on the fucking phone at the asscrack of dawn?"

"Logan."

"Why so early?"

"Oh, he had a damn good reason. Ronnie's not doing well and the scouts for ACM want to discuss possibly signing me."

"Really? What's the news with Ronnie?"

I fill her in on all of the details and we spend the next hour in bed discussing things. Ivy is always so positive and makes me see the light in every situation, when typically all I focus on is the bad. I'm the luckiest fucker ever.

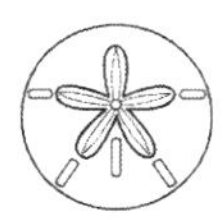

As we drive to the gym to pick up my check and talk to Logan in person, Ivy asks me, "Did they say when they wanna meet?"

"I don't think so, but I'd bet they are still in town, so maybe in the next few days."

She looks out the window, not responding; she's been in a bit of a daze since we left the house. "Hey, you okay?"

"Yeah, just thinking about Zoë."

"What about?" I ask, curious that she is on both of our minds so much today.

"She used to always talk about your fights, and I could hear how proud she was of you. I'm just sad that she's not here to be a part of this."

Reaching over, I take her hand and wrap it in mine. "Baby, she's always with us."

Ivy blinks back tears and I bring her knuckles to my lips, kissing them as I pull into a parking spot. Putting the truck in park, I pat my chest and she unbuckles her seatbelt scooting closer to me.

"Don't cry, babe." I hold on to her, but my words won't help. She sobs into my chest and I wonder what set her off so quickly. "Shhhh." I try and calm her down.

She looks at me shaking her head and says, "Are we crazy for thinking that…" She lets out a big breath of air. "That we could run from the past and make this work?"

I don't like where her line of thinking is going one bit. "Of course we're crazy, we all are in our own ways, but it doesn't make what we're doing wrong. Nothing or no one can stop this," I point between the two of us, "Or make things not work, except for you. I'm in this for the long haul, Ivy, and I want you by my side. I don't want to imagine my life without you." She blinks away the tears. My words stun her. She keeps listening to me and I continue. "Please let go of the past and hold on to what's real." I place her hand over my heart as it pounds fiercely against the walls of my chest. "This is what the thought of losing you does to me."

She leaves her hand on my heart and says, "I don't want to lose you."

"You won't. Now be strong for me, like you always have."

"I'm trying, but sometimes I get lost in my own thoughts and worries."

Leaning down, I kiss her tender lips, looking in her eyes for the reassurance that I need right now. "Don't do that." She kisses me back, giving me a little smile and asks, "Do you mind if I stay in the car?"

"Of course not, I'll be right out."

Leaving the keys in the ignition, I hop out and walk into the gym. "What's up, man?" Ethan calls and the guys all begin clapping for me. "Stop it," I respond, waving them off.

"Not much, any news on Ronnie?" I ask, shaking Ethan's hand.

"Nothing new."

"Damn, where's Logan?"

"On the phone with ACM – things seem to be really serious with their interest in you."

"What do you mean?" I ask catching sight of

Logan pacing in the back of the gym. He is gripping the back of his neck, like he's stressed, nodding his head repeatedly.

"He's been on the phone with them on and off for almost an hour."

I look at Ethan, not believing him, but can see he's dead serious.

"Wow, so this could really happen, couldn't it?"

"Yeah, man, but you have to stop beating yourself up about Ronnie."

"I know I do," I tell him, "It's just hard."

"Have a little faith, brother, he'll get better. Listen, sorry about walking in on you and Ivy last night."

"It's all good."

"What's the deal with you two anyway?" he asks curiously.

I haven't told any of them that we are actually dating yet, not that it's a secret or anything, but things have evolved so quickly and the fight was sprung on me so fast that I didn't have the time. "We're together."

"Good for you, man."

"Who's together?" Logan asks approaching the counter.

"Ivy and I."

"I knew it," he says. "I mean, I didn't know it, but I suspected it. She make you happy?"

"Yeah, she does, man."

"That's all that matters, brother."

Raising my chin to him I ask, "So what's the word?"

"Man, shit's moving fast. They want to fly us out to Vegas. Today."

"What? Why Vegas?"

"I guess the scouts left last night and that's where they are headquartered."

"Okay. If we go, how long will we be gone for and what's it going to entail?"

"From what it sounds like, possibly a contract. I mean, we won't know 'til we're there, but they said they'd send their private jet and have all the accommodations handled for an overnight trip."

"Can Ivy come?"

"I'm sure. I'm waiting on an email and I'll ask in my response."

"Cool, I'll talk to Ivy about it now, but we should be good. I'll text you." He hands me the check for last night's fight and I shake both of their hands before leaving. Walking out I open the check and blink a few times looking at it. Turning back to Logan and Ethan, I ask, “Why is this so much?” Logan walks to me and I hand it to him.

“Probably to show their interest in you,” he responds.

With the check in hand, I walk out looking at the amount one more time. What I thought would be seven thousand dollars is seventeen thousand. ACM just gave me an extra ten grand for no reason.

Chapter 24

"Are we really doing this?" Ivy asks as we pull out of the bank drive thru and head to the airport to meet Logan and Victoria.

I look behind us and see our suitcases resting on the backseat. "Looks like it."

"What if they don't offer you a contract?" she asks concerned.

"Then it wasn't meant to be, babe, and we got a free trip out of the deal."

"I really can't wait to get away," she says.

"Me too."

A text comes through her phone and she rolls her eyes. I glance down seeing it's her mom. "You know, you have to let go of the anger you have against her. Regardless of what blame she holds on me, she's your mom."

"She's never going to let go of what happened with Zoë."

"Then help her do it. Give her a reason to see why she needs to."

Ivy nods her head and begins to text her mom back. Pulling off the freeway, with the sun shining high in the sky, I think about what I am about to embark on. Today could be the first step towards the rest of my life, towards a real future in the MMA world. No more last minute underground fights for chump change. Regardless of what happens with Ronnie, I cannot carry that burden. I have to believe that he will be fine. That he'll pull through and my family will be safe, like they've always been.

The possibilities for the future are great, and for that, I'm one lucky bastard. I could be making good money, where Ivy would never have to work again, and I can give her the future that she deserves.

"She wants to have dinner."

"Who?" I ask confused, my daydream cut short.

"My mom."

"With you?"

"With both of us."

"When?"

"She didn't say, but I basically told her that

we are dating."

"Whoa, whoa, whoa. What exactly did you say to her, Ivy?"

"I told her earlier that she's been making me miserable and she flew off the handle, so I ignored her." I glare at her, as much as her mom pisses me off, she really has no one left except for Ivy.

"Let me just read it to you," she says and scrolls through her messages with her eyebrows scrunched together. "Mom, yes, I have been ignoring you but for a reason—the words that you said to Krane yesterday were hurtful. He has been amazing to me and has helped me in so many ways that you'd never understand. He's shown me how to be strong and to cope with the loss of Zoë. I can see the pain that he's gone through losing her and for you to blame him, it's not fair. During everything that we've gone through together, we've grown close. Granted none of us knows what the future will hold, but I know that mine will have Krane in it. So if you want to be part of my life, then you need to let go of the resentment that you have against him and be a part of his life too."

I swallow hard after hearing her words and

realize how much I've helped her. I mean, I can remember times right after Zoë passed that she was a wreck and I had to force her to be strong. I'd talk to her 'til she fell asleep and then call her in the morning when I got up to wake her, forcing her out of bed. But I was drunk most of the time, so I didn't realize then the impact that I was having on her. Thinking about those times makes me realize how she's changed me too. When I'm with Ivy, drinking is the last thing on my mind. I don't even have a desire to do it, as long as she is with me.

"You really feel that way, about the future?"

"Yeah. I don't want to face it without you. I've tried and it's ugly. I'm not myself when we are apart; you've shown me the Ivy that I'm supposed to be."

Parking the truck at the airport, I turn it off and look over at her. I know that I'm not myself when we are apart either. "Ivy…I love you." I didn't plan on telling her this, but when it hits me, telling her is one of the easiest things I've ever done.

She smiles from ear to ear and takes my hand placing it over her heart. "I love you, Krane." Her heart pounds profusely and she says, "This is what you do to me any time that we're together."

Bringing her lips to mine, I study her eyes and wonder how in the world I got so lucky…again. I hesitate for a second before kissing her and ask, "Ready to see what the future will hold?" She answers me with a kiss and then we hop out of the truck.

Grabbing our bags, I see the ACM plane right away. It is wrapped in graphics with their company logo and sponsors, making it stick out more than any other plane on the tarmac. Logan waves from the door, popping his head out. "Holy shit," Ivy says excitedly. We head that way and I can't help but look at her. She looks different – calmer – happier.

Walking to the stairs, I lead Ivy up in front of me. Inside, two flight attendants greet us, handing us two glasses of Champagne as they take our bags and the two pilots in the cockpit wave at us.

"Will there be anyone else?" one of the attendants asks Logan.

"No, ma'am."

Victoria and Ivy hug all giddy and excited. I take a look around the plane as I fist bump Logan. "Man, this is unreal."

"I know, right? Here, let's sit down, I have a lot to go over with you."

We take a seat and he hands me a folder of paperwork, and says, "These are stipulations, if you do sign. They want you to review everything now."

There has to be over fifty pages here. As I flip through skimming it, there are all sorts of different things, a section for approved fight apparel, marketing clauses, a slew of different bonuses.

Fuck, this is a lot.

"What are we thinking going into this with just the two of us?" I close the packet and hand it back to him.

The stewardess walks by and I stop her. "Could I have a shot of tequila, please?" I have got to steady my nerves. Even Ivy's calming powers can't battle the swarm rising in my stomach.

Logan glares at me and interrupts her, "He'll take a bottle of water. Krane, you agreed to let me manage you. I'm not going to let you go into the biggest meeting of your life drunk."

"What's the difference? Drunk or not, we're not prepared to do this. Have you read any of this?"

"Yeah, every page, and I spoke to ACM about some concerns I already have. That's why I want to go over it with you now."

"Regardless of concerns, we need someone with a legal background to look over anything before I sign it." I glance at Ivy and she nods her head in agreement.

"They will have an attorney present to work out everything, they are prepared to negotiate and are dead serious about bringing you into their fighting family. If you would stop being so fucking difficult and trust me, you'd see that I can do this and am prepared to make sure you get a sweet deal."

"Umm, an attorney for *their* side, not mine, but I'll trust you. And what about Ronnie?"

"He has nothing to do with your deal. It was an unfortunate outcome, but you're not liable in any way. Would you let that go, man?"

I take Ivy's hand and wrap it in mine. I move my eyes to the window and zone out Logan's stare. It's not that I don't want to. I can't. My head is all over the place…maybe I'm not ready to do this.

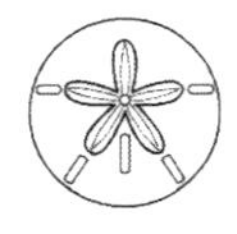

I just need five minutes alone with Ivy to set my head straight.

After the plane landed in Vegas, a private car picked us up to take us to the meeting with ACM. Logan and I discussed things the entire flight, but nothing he's said has sold me on doing this. I feel like I am about to sign my life away and that scares me. What if I end up like Ronnie?

"You okay?" Ivy asks, kissing my neck. I nod my head looking at her for something, anything to get me through this.

"Okay, they are all ready for us," Logan says hanging up his phone. The car comes to a stop and the driver opens the rear door.

"I need to talk to you," I whisper to Ivy. Then Logan gets out first and I follow.

"Hey, man, can I have a few minutes alone with Ivy?" I ask before proceeding.

"Sure, I'll let them know we're here."

Logan walks off and I guide Ivy out of the car, she takes my hands looking into my eyes as they follow his back. "What's going though your head?"

"How do I know this is the right thing to do?"

"Look at me," bringing my face to hers. "You know as well as I do that nothing is guaranteed in life, everything could end tomorrow. This might be your only opportunity at a real fighting career, so you've gotta go in there with an open mind and at least explore the options."

"I hear ya, but what if I sign a contract and get injured fighting or they require me to move somewhere to train?"

"You know that this job comes with a great risk, but you've got the best angel watching over you. I believe that Zoë will keep you safe. And if you move, I move. I'll go where you go. That should be the least of your worries. You gotta have faith in us, in me. Stop thinking stupid thoughts. Are you in this for the long haul?" I nod my head, taking in her words of encouragement. "Well, you know I am. This deal could change your life for the better, it could give you the future that you've always dreamed of. Zoë would want you to do this. So listen to me when I tell you that I am not going anywhere and I will support whatever you decide, because I fucking love you, Krane Hensley."

Logan opens the door and whistles for me, "Let's go, man."

Leaning in, I kiss Ivy, knowing that no matter what happens, I'll have her in the end.

Chapter 25

"How are you gonna tell Ivy?" Logan asks me as we walk to the elevator in our hotel.

"I'm not, my face will tell her everything."

He presses the elevator call button and I exhale. "Damn, I need a drink," I say as we step inside.

"You and me both."

"You know, if we'd brought our own attorney that would have probably been done in half the time." It's after eight; the meeting lasted over three hours. Thank God the girls checked into the rooms rather than sitting there and waiting for us. As the doors open to the twenty-second floor, Logan points to the direction that we are headed and says, "Here you are, twenty-two eleven," as we approach my room.

"Thanks for today," I tell him as he walks off.

"You can buy me a drink later," he says from down the hall. I knock on the door of the hotel room and wait for Ivy to open it. It's not but a few seconds and her sparkling eyes meet mine. I step inside and she beams from ear to ear in excitement, waiting for me to tell her the news. But I don't do that and my flat expression changes everything. She scrunches her eyebrows at me and asks, "What happened, what's wrong?"

"Nothing," I say, pulling her body to mine and brushing my lips tenderly against hers.

"Nothing happened, or nothing's wrong?" she asks pulling her head further back looking me in the eye again. I smirk holding her closer, and press my lips to her neck.

She pushes me away, her demeanor filled with concern, and grabs my hand lifting up my right sleeve and then the left. When she finds the diamond-encrusted watch on my left wrist, she about slaps me. "You got fuckin' signed?"

Slowly I nod, watching how she absorbs the news and how right away it makes her ecstatic. A huge grin breaks out across my face. "Why didn't you just tell me?"

"I was playing. Plus, I needed to make sure you wouldn't run for the hills."

"Jesus Christ, Krane, you are such an ass." She slaps my chest and I hold her wrists, her eyes getting wide when I control her like this. Looking down at my hundred-grand watch, it gleams in the light. I wasn't even looking for a hundred-grand contract. I just wanted enough to survive, but ACM is no joke – they are the top of the top and gave me way more than that.

"Well, I'm your ass." I slip the watch off and put it on her.

"You are," she says smiling and flattens her hands on my chest, staring at the diamond Rolex. I let go of her wrists and she says, "Give me all the details."

"Everything?" I ask.

"Yes, especially all of the important parts."

"Umm, my first fight is in two months."

"Against who?"

"Some new up and comer, should be easy from what Logan knows of him."

"Where will it be?"

"They said Toronto, so you better get your passport ready." She raises her eyebrows at me, liking the idea of traveling. "Logan will stay on as my primary trainer, I'll fight out of Ethan's gym, and if I want, ACM could get me set up with one of their camps to try out. But I told them that right now I don't want to move, and they don't have any camps in New York."

"Wow, it sounds like you got everything you wanted."

"Yeah, I mean, the money is gonna change our life, and the small things like the appearances and required fight apparel, I'll learn to deal with."

"So how much did you get?"

"A half a million fucking signing bonus baby, plus I'll get fifty thousand for every fight to start. If I win, there's a bonus too." Ivy's eyes gloss over with tears hearing the news.

"I'm so proud of you," she says.

"Thanks, and the real bonus is it sounds like Ronnie is gonna be okay. He started to move his toes today and the feeling is coming back in his legs."

"Thank God." She hugs me tightly.

"I can't wait to give you the world, baby."

"You already have."

"I couldn't have done any of this without you. Thank you for pushing me."

She reaches down unbuttoning my shirt and says, "Any time. So why don't you pay me back?"

"I'd love to."

"You know, I like you dressed like this."

"I bet you do." I guide her backwards with my body and hover over her, grinding my cock against her sex. "Don't get used to it though 'cause it's not gonna last."

She removes my shirt and I push hers upwards. Never getting tired of seeing her gorgeous body. I growl at the sight of her nipples and pinch one of them hard before clamping it in between my teeth. "Oh fuck," she whines in pleasure, unzipping my pants.

I push against her hand; my cock needs the friction. I need to be inside of her. I want her. Finally, she gets my pants undone and I kick them off. Pulling her underwear to the side, I don't waste one second before I clench the base of my shaft and slam into her.

Growling as her warm pussy accepts me, I work our bodies, stroking myself in and out of her. "Take my cock, baby."

She grips for the sheets to try to hold steady, which sets me off. The way her body twists and moves, her noises, my cock riding her, it all puts me into overdrive and then I realize there is no need to rush. Yes, I can be rough, but in my own way. So I take my time, slowing things down a bit.

Pulling out of her, she looks at me concerned. "Come here," I tell her and guide her to her knees. As we both kneel facing each other, I take the hem of her shirt and slowly lift it over her head. She watches my hands and how I undress her.

With one of her tits so perfectly in my mouth, I reach beneath her panties where her tight wet cunt waits for me. Sinking two fingers inside of her, I pull away and watch how her eyes contract from being under my control. "I love you, Ivy."

"I love you. Are you okay?" she asks worried by my change in pace.

"Yeah, I just want to show you how much you mean to me."

She looks down at our bodies, me with my fingers inside of her and my hard cock dripping pre-cum as I wait to fuck her again. "I think you were. Why did you stop?"

I remove my hand from her panties and she glares at me. "Like that, why are you stopping?"

"I felt like I was rushing things, which maybe I do sometimes because I lost Zoë and am afraid of losing you too."

"I'm not going anywhere, baby."

"You don't know that."

"Thinking of the past, I guess I don't. But if my time does come, I want to go after you've fucked me rough and dirty, the way that I like. I love it when you push my panties to the side or bite my nipples. Please don't change who you are, okay?"

I nod and take my thumb, flicking it over her tit. She grabs my cock bringing my eyes to follow the movements of her hand.

Christ, she strokes me so good.

Tilting my head back, I close my eyes and grunt out.

Her soft lips find my neck where she kisses a trail up to my ear and then whispers, "Fuck me hard, Krane."

Taking my hand to hers, I stop her from stroking my shaft. The blood pumps to the tip, making me so stiff. My breathing is ragged and with my eyes as serious as ever, I flip her over and land one hard smack to her plump white ass. She yelps and shakes it for me to do it again. Pulling her panties out of the way, I hover over her. My cock is lined up with her pussy and her breathing has stopped as she waits for me.

"Tell me what you want."

"I want you to fuck me hard."

"I bet you do." I nudge my dick against her and she pushes towards me. I pull away, teasing her and ask, "How do you want me to fuck you?"

She's breathing again and in between labored breaths, her head is hung low as she is on all fours and says, "Hard and rough, 'til I come."

With her words, I bury myself inside of her. Sitting back up, just on my knees, I keep ahold of her ass cheeks as I work her. The room is filled with the noises of our skin slapping together. Her outstretched body glistens with sweat and she screams my name.

Landing a firm hit to the other side of her ass, I tell her, "Let me hear you."

My command sets her off and in this moment, we are both lost. Lost from all reality. Nothing matters right now, but satisfying her. As the noises echo in the room and I watch myself moving in and out of her, I know I've never been happier.

A knock on the door startles me, but nothing can stop us. Drilling her deep, I let go grunting low as she screams into the comforter. "Yesssss, come on my cock," I murmur probably a little too loudly, but nothing that we are doing is a secret.

"Krane," Logan says through the door and knocks again.

"One sec!" I shout, spanking her as I pull my pants back on. Ivy giggles and before I open the door to the room, I see her sexy ass run into the bathroom.

Chapter 26

"I want another shot!" Ivy yells, drunk off her ass and I can't help but laugh at the fit she's throwing.

"No!" I shake my head and pull her onto my lap. The club we are at is crowded and loud, but somehow Logan scored us a VIP table, which gives us some privacy.

"You know, you're really controlling sometimes," she says crossing her arms over her chest.

"You like it!"

She rests her head on my shoulder and settles back. "Is it because Zoë died after drinking a lot?" she asks.

"Stop it! It's because I don't want you to feel like shit tomorrow."

"How could I, waking up next to you?"

"Oh you could, alcohol will make you feel like…" I trail off and get lost in her eyes as they stare at me. Pulling away, I look out at the dance floor. Logan and Victoria are in the middle of a swarm of people dancing away, which is not my scene. I prefer to be here, with Ivy in my arms.

"Like what?" she asks.

"Huh?"

"What will alcohol make me feel like?" she slurs, sitting back staring at me, her glossy eyes so gorgeous and tired.

Oh, she's drunk.

I direct her to stand. "Come on, let's get you some fresh air, beautiful."

"I don't need it."

"Yes, you do."

We leave the club together, the music behind us muffles as the hot Vegas air wraps around our bodies and we walk down to a huge lake with a lit up water show. Standing together, I have my arm around Ivy, both of us watching the sight in front of us. Then her head starts to hang low, she's quiet, and it makes me nervous. The world around me halts, taking me back to the subway ride home the night I lost Zoë not so long ago.

Lifting her chin, I look into her eyes, needing to know that she's okay. But there are tears glossed over them. Pulling her close to my chest,

I hold her tight and ask, "What's the matter?"

"Nothing, I'm just happy."

"Then don't cry."

She nods her head and I catch sight of Logan and Victoria as they walk down the sidewalk. He has his arm around her and is whispering into her ear.

"I mean it, baby, enjoy every second we have together, don't waste tears on any of it." I glance over at Logan as he catches sight of me and he raises his chin. When they approach, he passes Ivy a bottle of water.

"Would everyone stop acting like I'm drunk?"

"We would, if you weren't drunk," he says.

She rolls her eyes and says, "You guys suck."

"Yes, you do," I tease her and she bumps me with her shoulder. "Ready to head back?"

We all agree and decide to walk.

"Have you guys ever been to Vegas?" Victoria asks us. We both shake our heads and she says, "Logan and I love it, we almost got married here."

"Shut up!" Ivy exclaims, "I'd love a Vegas wedding!"

"You would?" I ask completely taken off

guard by this bomb.

"Yeah! I wouldn't have to take months out of my life planning it, not to mention how stress-free it would be."

"Isn't that what girls want, all the planning?" Logan asks.

"Some...maybe, but not me," Ivy says.

I'm sure for Ivy a Vegas wedding would be better, especially since she lost her father as a teenager in a car accident and without Zoë around, I can see where she is coming from. Up ahead there is a wedding chapel. As a young couple emerges through the front doors laughing and holding hands, it sparks something inside of me.

I've lived this life with too many fucking regrets. Too much lost time. I don't want that anymore. If Ivy's dream is to have a Vegas wedding, then I'll give her one. With my hand wrapped tightly around hers, I watch the way her eyes sparkle in the light of the sign.

Turning her to face me, I get down on one knee. Logan and Victoria jolt to a stop, looking at us, shocked. Ivy's hand flies over her mouth as she looks down at me and I push away the rest of the world.

"Ivy Amaranth Winslow, I love you more than anything in this world. My heart was broken for so long before you. But now I have a purpose. You're my reason for existence; you have shown me what it's like to love again. I know our love is just beginning, but we found each other for a reason. And I don't want to miss out on starting our future." With the biggest grin I've ever had on my face, I bring her sweet hand to my lips and ask, "Ivy, will you marry me tonight, right here and right now?"

She starts nodding her head before I can even finish my sentence and I kiss her soft ring finger, wishing I had a fucking ring to put on it. Standing up, she throws her arms over my shoulders and kisses me harder than I've ever felt. Then clapping and whistles ring around us, as a crowd gathered watching the proposal.

As I hold her tightly and inhale her sweet scent, I bury my face into the comfort of her neck, so grateful that for once in my life, everything is going according to plan.

Chapter 27

Stretching my arms high above my head, I let out a yawn. My hand hits the headboard and the sound of the metal hitting the wood, takes me back to last night. Blinking a few times, I take in the room and then lift my hand in front of my face.

Staring back at me is indeed a wedding band. The events all flood through my mind and each make me smile. From the proposal, to the cheesy Elvis impersonator, to Ivy walking down the aisle and then saying those two little words, *I do.*

Rolling over, she is passed out. The skin of her exposed shoulder draws my lips to it and I search for her left hand where an extravagant ring sparkles. Taking her hand in mine, I hold on to it and cuddle her close. As I fiddle with the diamond, she wrestles awake. "Morning," I whisper into her ear.

She moans stretching and catches me touching her ring. Suddenly she flies out of bed naked. Standing there staring, breathing heavily, she looks at the ring on her left hand. "Oh my God, Krane, what did we do?"

Tilting my head shocked, I'm not sure what to say or how to talk her off of the ledge right now.

"Don't you remember?" I ask, scared of her answer.

"I was drunk!" she shouts.

"Fuck!" I shout sitting up and run my hand over my face.

She chants, "No! No! No! No! No! No! No! Please tell me we didn't."

I'm thrown off by her response. But don't have a choice but to be honest and nod, "We did."

"Dammit!"

"Come on, Ivy, you weren't that drunk."

She looks at me and then at her ring. "I know, I remember it all and loved every second of it." Her face morphs into a huge grin. She was just fucking with me. Grabbing her by the waist, I toss her onto the bed.

"Why would you do that to me?"

"Payback for fucking with me when you got signed. Plus, I needed to make sure you wouldn't run for the hills." She uses my words on me again, and I can't even respond.

"So you remember it all?"

"Yes, stupid, I told you I wasn't drunk! Krane, last night you made my dreams come true. I'm the luckiest woman in the world."

"So no regrets or reservations?"

"Nope, none for me. Convincing my mom is going to be rather difficult, but we'll do it together."

"I think I have something in mind."

The phone in the room rings and I answer it. "How are the newlyweds doing?" Logan asks.

"We're good, just working through our re-grets, that's all."

"Shut the fuck up."

"I'm joking. What's up?"

"Victoria and I were gonna head down for breakfast before checkout, you guys wanna join?"

My free hand roams Ivy's body settling on her sex. Pushing my finger in her slit I respond, "Yeah, brother, we'll be down in a few minutes."

Ivy glares at me as I work her pussy and then I stretch my body over her as I hang the phone up. "You better be joking."

"Oh, like you were this morning?" I raise my eyebrows at her and sink a finger inside of her. She moans and I stroke her insides, watching how much she enjoys it, twisting and writhing beneath me. Then I pull away and hop up, grabbing a pair of shorts from my bag.

"Oh my God, are you serious?" she yells, angry and horny.

"Yup, payback's a bitch. Come on, Logan and Victoria are waiting for us."

She moves her hand down her body, touching herself, knowing that this is my weak spot. "Oh, no, you don't," I rip the covers off of her and pull her hand away. "Get dressed."

"You can't tell me what to do." She squeezes her tits looking at me with those eyes.

"The fuck I can't; you're my wife. Now get your sexy ass dressed and don't touch my pussy again unless I give you permission." I take my toothbrush and toothpaste into the bathroom, watching her get out of bed in the reflection of the mirror. She's frustrated, but it feels so good to play with her like this. I can already see our life together is gonna be a shit ton of fun and I couldn't be happier.

Chapter 28

"What did you think of him?" Logan asks me after our meeting with a new potential boxing coach.

"He seems good. What did you think?"

"I like him. He's worked with some of the best boxers in the world. I think he can get you to where you need to be striking wise over the next few months."

Since returning from Vegas, Logan and I started our training routine and have been hitting the gym harder then ever.

My phone rings, sitting on the edge of the mat. "Hang on one second," I tell Logan.

"Mr. Hensley," a familiar voice says, "This is Will from the Terrace. I wanted to let you know that everything for this evening is in order." I'm stoked for tonight and know that Ivy is going to be thrilled when I take her there. She mentioned this place in passing a while ago and had no idea I was taking notes then.

"Perfect, we'll be there about six o'clock."

"I'll see you then, Mr. Hensley." I hang up with him and dial Ivy.

"Hey, baby," she answers breathlessly.

"Hey, what are you up to?" I ask.

"Not much, just wrapping up things at my apartment."

"Did you talk to your mom about tonight?" I ask.

"Uhh, not exactly."

"What does that mean?" I ask, getting a little annoyed that communicating with her mom is so difficult.

"I told her we'd like to have dinner with her tonight. And she said she'd think about it. She's having a hard time accepting things."

Since Ivy broke the news to her mom of our Vegas wedding everything has changed. She's no longer willing to work past our differences.

"I'm sorry, baby."

"It's not your fault."

"Yeah, it kinda is."

"No, it's not. Don't even go there. I'll call her later after she has some time to cool down."

"Okay, you still up for lunch?"

"Absolutely, I need a break."

We hang up and I stare at the screen on my phone, a picture of Ivy and I the morning after we got married looks back at me. I don't want this all to fall on her shoulders. She shouldn't be having to deal with this from her own mother. Stepping out back of the gym, I dial Brenda's number. We haven't spoken since the day that she and I argued on the phone a few weeks back.

"Hello?"

"Hi Brenda, it's Krane." She doesn't respond, clearly not happy with me, so I continue doing what I called for. "Brenda, I know you aren't a fan of mine, but just hear me out, for Ivy?"

She's still silent and I look at the screen to see she hasn't hung up.

"Ivy is really upset with what your relationship has become. We both love her a great deal and what you're doing to her is torture. Don't make what should be the happiest time in her life miserable. Please, have dinner with us tonight. We'll be at the Terrace in Long Beach and then you can see yourself that I love her and make her happy."

The line is silent and I know this time she

hung up. There's really nothing more that I can do. If Brenda is going to hold on to her hatred for me over her love for Ivy, then I just need to make Ivy happy and keep her mind off of her mother.

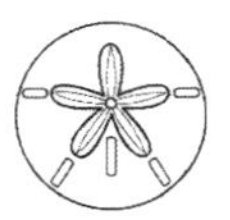

"Are people staring at us?" Ivy asks, sitting next to me blindfolded as we drive to dinner.

"No, of course not," I chuckle. "This is normal for New York." She throws her arm at me to hit me and I grab it. "I might have to blindfold you more often if you're gonna be this feisty."

I keep glancing at her as we drive. Her hands are placed so neatly in her lap. She keeps looking around like she can see through the blindfold. Which I know she can't. I only used it to keep her mind busy, off of the negative shit with her mom.

She's upset that her mom bailed on tonight, but I'm hoping my surprise will make up for it. Brenda sent her a text message and said she couldn't come. It pissed me off, so I texted her myself and laid into her saying some things that I'll never be able to take back. But at least I stood up for Ivy and now she knows how I really feel.

Pulling up to the Terrace, I remove the blindfold. She smiles the second that she sees where we are. As we exit the truck, I hand the keys to the valet and walk around taking Ivy's hand in mine, never getting tired of how her ring feels against my skin. "You remembered."

"Of course I did. I remember everything you say."

The hostess seats us at a table overlooking the vast ocean view of Long Beach, a place that has become both of our favorites.

Taking Ivy's hands in mine over the table, she looks at me with so much love and adoration. "Thank you for coming out with me tonight. I know it's hard that your mom isn't accepting things."

She smiles and nods, squeezing my hands. "It's okay. I have to learn to let it go."

"Nah, she'll come around, I'm sure of it."

"Maybe, but for tonight, can we not talk about her anymore? If she wanted to be here, she could."

"Of course." I take her hand and bring it to

my lips. She touches my cheek and asks, "How was training today?" rubbing her thumb under a small cut I got from sparring today.

"It was good. Logan's bringing on a new boxing coach, so between Logan and him, I should be more than prepared for my next fight."

"I have no doubt you will."

The waiter takes our drink order and we continue our conversation. "That's the plan. Did I tell you Ling called and wanted me to take a fight tonight?"

"Shut up!"

"I'm serious, I guess he didn't get busted after all."

"What did you tell him?"

"I told him about my contract with ACM and he said no one would ever know if I kept fighting with him."

"Oh my God!"

"I know, so I hung up and blocked his phone number. I don't even want ACM to think I'm talking to someone like that."

"You told them that you used to fight underground, right?"

"Yeah."

The waiter sets our drinks down and as he turns away, both Ivy and I are shocked to see her mom standing at the table.

"Mom!" she blurts out stunned. "I didn't think you were coming."

"I wasn't," Brenda adds drily.

"We're so glad you're here," I respond hoping that we can settle this shit with her once and for all. I gesture her to sit and she does right across from me.

Taking Ivy's hand in mine on top of the table, I squeeze it to give her some reassurance. The metal of my wedding band catches Brenda's eye and she looks off, taking in a deep breath of air.

She looks down, like she's holding back tears while we wait for her to say something.

"Mom, Krane makes me really happy." Ivy takes her other hand and grabs her mom's.

She nods, trying to keep the tears at bay. "I can see that." She looks at me briefly and then back at her. "I arrived before you both did tonight and watched you interact. It's not that I don't want to accept this, I'm just having a hard time understanding how the two of you can act like Zoë never existed."

"Why would say that?" Ivy asks, clearly hurt by her mom's words.

"Why wouldn't I?"

"Brenda, Ivy and I both love Zoë and miss her so much."

"If you did, then you wouldn't have gotten married."

"That's not even fair to say," Ivy says. "I fell in love with Krane, the same way that you fell in love with Daddy, you can't control that."

"Don't compare him to the man your father was, Ivy."

"No, Mom, I will. Krane has been the most amazing man in my life since I lost Daddy. Why do you think we're having dinner in Long Beach?" She shrugs her shoulders and Ivy says, "Don't you remember every summer that we spent here growing up? This was Zoë's favorite place in the entire world, and the night she passed, she'd asked Krane to take her here the following day."

"She did?" Brenda asks stunned at learning this new information.

"She did," I confirm. "But unfortunately that never happened and we all know why. However, I still came and continued every morning for six months. Then one day, I brought Ivy here and I shared the story with her. Brenda, it wasn't long until I fell in love with Ivy, right out there on that beach." I point to the dark sand lit by the moon. "We both have a hard time believing that wasn't Zoë pushing the two of us together."

Ivy and her mother are both crying. This is not the way that I saw this evening going, but all I can do now is try and salvage it. "You don't have to like me, or even accept me. But please, don't take your anger out on Ivy." Brenda nods once, and turns to pull Ivy into a hug. I take this moment to slip away and give them a few minutes alone.

Walking to the front of the Terrace, I look out at the beautiful place and catch sight of Will walking into the restaurant. He walks to me and says, "How's dinner?"

"I'm not sure we'll be eating."

"Is everything okay?"

"Yeah, just a little family drama."

"I'm so sorry."

"It's okay."

"While I have you alone, here are your keys." He passes me the ring of silver keys and pats my back. "Congratulations."

"Thanks." I shake his hand and look over at Ivy as she and her mom are talking. She sees me and waves me back to them. Walking back to the table, I place my hand on Ivy's back. "Are you guys okay?"

"Yeah we are."

Brenda looks at the both of us and says, "I'm sorry for the things I've said and for the way I've acted."

"I think we all are. But the past is the past. Eat dinner with us, Brenda, and let this be a clean fresh start."

She agrees and right away I can see the smile growing on Ivy's face. This is going to take a lot of work to break down her walls, but for Ivy, I'll do anything.

Chapter 29

After saying goodbye to her mom, I press the elevator call button, the doors chime open, and I usher Ivy inside.

"Where are we going?" she asks holding my hand tightly, watching me press the button for the twenty-first floor.

"Home."

The elevator soars to the top floor and I can only imagine what is going through Ivy's mind. As we walk down the hall, I reach into my pocket pulling out the keys. With them clutched tightly in the palm of my hand, we stop in front of the white door with a plaque on the side that reads twenty-one hundred.

Opening my hand, I show Ivy the keys. Her expression is priceless. I love the immediate excitement that comes across her face. "Welcome home, baby."

Slowly she takes the keys that I pass to her and slides one of them into the lock. Effortlessly it turns and then I open the door to our new condo. The big open floor plan is spectacular, but the wall of glass windows that overlook the beach is the icing on the cake.

Ivy spins to me, astonished, and throws her arms around my neck.

"How does it feel to be standing in the middle of our new home?"

"Krane, I'm…" She knots her fingers together behind my neck. "I'm speechless."

"Good, that's what I was hoping for."

"This place is amazing and the view." She walks to the window of the balcony. "Did you really mean what you said earlier about falling in love with me down there?" She points to the spot we stopped on one of our morning runs and I can remember the instant like it was yesterday.

"Of course I did. At the time, I might not have admitted it to myself, but I know that's when it happened."

As we stand together and look out at the sight that we will share for the rest of our lives, I hold her close, her back firmly against the front of my chest, and I breathe her in, so turned on by the simple scent that she exudes. She reaches back, gripping my neck and grinds her ass against me. I push my cock into her, needing her.

Turning her face towards mine, my mouth finds hers and I claim her lips. The lips of my wife. "Mmm," she moans and I don't think I've ever enjoyed a kiss more. Taking the straps of her dress, I push both of them over her shoulders and watch as the smooth fabric glides down her body, pooling in a pile at her feet. Stepping back, I flick the light off and admire her white lace bra and panties with the moonlight shining in the room.

"So beautiful," I whisper, running my hands over her curves. She cups my dick, turning me on, and I respond by tearing the side of her underwear. "Sorry." She laughs, and then I rip them all of the way off of her.

Taking her time, she undresses me, our mouths attacking one another, which makes it harder to get naked.

God, I love her.

Taking her bottom lip in between my teeth, I tug up and look her in the eye. The connection we share is a straight line to the tip of my dick. Her kisses connect right to it.

"Bra off!" She unclasps it as I completely remove my pants. "Turn around," I order her. She complies with my request, giving me the greatest view in the world. Her body a silhouette against the backdrop of the midnight sky bound by the moonlight. Stroking my hard shaft, I reach around her body and spread her pussy nudging my way inside of her, inch by inch. She leans back grasping me and I whisper into her skin "I love you."

In between a moan from the pleasure of my dick, she responds, "I love you."

As our bodies rock together, I push myself so hard into her, not showing any mercy with my long thrusts. I know that no matter what happens in my lifetime, Ivy is who I am meant to be with. Everything that I've endured up to this point, all of the pain and heartache that I have lived through was to get me here – to this moment – with her.

I don't care if I lose my next fight or fail completely at a MMA career, because I know that Ivy will always be waiting for me. Pressing my fingers into her skin, I hold her tight, leaving an indentation, marking her in my own way.

Being with her has healed me.

Ivy is the mirror to my soul.

Pumping my cock strongly inside of her sweet heavenly cunt, my eyes are pulled out to the ocean and the spot where I fell in love with her. I am confident that what we have will last forever. Until the ocean runs dry and the moon gives its last flicker of light. She's mine.

Acknowledgements

As I sit here and write these acknowledgements, they never get easier. This is truly the hardest part of a book as an author. There might only be a few hundred words, but to get it right and acknowledge everyone is...difficult. There is so much that goes into making a book perfect and so many amazing people who help.

As always, my Prezident, I love you more than any words can ever say. You are the king of my world. I am completely and utterly blessed to have you by my side as we complete another book. I have to give you props for *3 Breaths*, so much of the storyline you helped me with and like usual, you read the book more than I did. Thanks, baby, for everything, from the bottom of my heart. I am the luckiest damn girl in the whole entire world.

Lisa, Lisa, Lisa, the amazing and remarkable

Lisa! I'm not really sure how to sum up my gratitude, but I'll try. You are simply a genius with words, you are fast and accurate as hell. You catch so many errors and always make the editing process fun. Thank you for always working with me. I love you, woman.

Letica and Janice, you two are the greatest proofreaders! Between the two of you, you make my life so easy. Thank you for going through *3 Breaths* in minute detail and catching all those final errors. I know I always give you like a day to read the entire book and not on purpose, but you come through and always amaze me. I couldn't do what I do without the two of you, that's for damn sure. Thank you for always having my back!

To the bloggers, I once thought that maybe I would start a blog. Then I realized everything that goes into it and knew I wasn't cut out for it. You have an extremely hard job that helps so many authors. Thank you for helping me, from signing up for the cover reveal to the release day blitz and blog tour. And for those of you that read the ARC and gave me feedback, your kind words have truly touched me. You know who you are—I am indebted to you always.

For my readers, like I said in the dedication page, this one is for you. So many of you have stuck by me since *Fatalism* and *Every Soul.* Thank you from the bottom of my heart for taking the time to read Krane and Ivy's story. I know this was a hard one! There were a lot of tears shed by the advanced readers, as there were by me as I wrote this story. But if you learned anything from Krane and Ivy, tomorrow is not guaranteed.

Take each breath as though it could be your last.

The Prezident and I read every single review, so we'd love to hear your thoughts. To stay up to date on the latest information regarding all of my books, please make sure that you sign up to stalk me on my website – www.authorlkcollins.com.

Printed in Great Britain
by Amazon